AF538429

Fourteen Hills

THE SAN FRANCISCO STATE UNIVERSITY REVIEW

Fourteen Hills

THE SAN FRANCISCO STATE UNIVERSITY REVIEW

No. 29
2023

Fourteen Hills Press
San Francisco, CA

Fourteen Hills would like to thank the following individuals and businesses for their kind support: Jane George, Katherine Kwid, Nona Caspers, May-lee Chai, Chet Wiener, the SFSU Poetry Center, Medicine for Nightmares Bookstore & Gallery, and the exceptional team at Bookmobile.

Thank you also to the Firehouse Fund for its generous support of *Fourteen Hills*.

Cover artwork: "Lost in the Grandeur" by Jewel Rodriguez.
Book design by James Giffin.

ISBN: 978-1-889292-84-7

Printed by Bookmobile, Inc. (Minneapolis, MN)
in the United States of America.

Published annually by Fourteen Hills Press:
San Francisco State University | Dept. of Creative Writing
1600 Holloway Ave | San Francisco CA 94132
www.14hills.net

Individual subscriptions are $16 for one year or $32 for two years. Back issues are $5 each. Visit https://fourteenhills.submittable.com, www.spdbooks.org (Small Press Distribution), or contact the publisher.

The submission period runs from February 15th to June 15th. All submissions are electronic via: https://fourteenhills.submittable.com. Additional details at www.14hills.net.

Erratum: in our previous issue, we misspelled the title of Megan Erickson's poem, "Le Macchine." Our sincerest apologies for the error.

THE SAN FRANCISCO STATE UNIVERSITY REVIEW

No. 29
2023

Awards Given Annually By *Fourteen Hills*

The **GINA BERRIAULT AWARD** was inaugurated by Peter Orner in conjunction with Fourteen Hills Press to pay homage to the eponymous writer, a former SFSU professor who with every story embodied a certain selflessness and unflinching compassion. The award is given annually to a writer with a similar spirit who has shown a love for storytelling and a commitment to helping young writers. Winning authors are honored with an award ceremony and reading, and their writing and/or an accompanying interview are featured in the newest issue of *Fourteen Hills.*

Stacy Doris was an Associate Professor in San Francisco State University's Creative Writing Department, where she taught for ten years. Her work as a translator and a poet is widely recognized. Doris was always creating new worlds with her unexpected poetics. Following upon that spirit of creative invention and inventive creation, the **STACY DORIS MEMORIAL POETRY AWARD** is given annually for a long poem with a truly inventive spirit. The winning poet receives $500 and publication of their winning poem in the upcoming issue of *Fourteen Hills.*

The **MICHAEL RUBIN BOOK AWARD** is an annual award named after the much-beloved SFSU professor Michael Rubin and is open to students and recent graduates of San Francisco State University. Alternating each year between poetry and fiction, manuscripts are gathered in an open competition and read by an independent guest judge. The winner must be an enrolled student or recent graduate of SFSU whose work shows exceptional accomplishment and promise. Traditionally, the winning manuscript has been published and promoted by Fourteen Hills Press, though the award's prize is currently in transition.

CONTENTS

No. 29 / 2023

SPECIAL FEATURE

INTERVIEW

VISUAL ART

CONTRIBUTORS

EDITOR'S STATEMENT: ON SAFETY, SAFETY PINS, AND THE SELF

Quinn Rennerfeldt Fairchild

As an editor, I am endlessly fascinated by the themes and subjects that swirl around in the collective subconscious. There seems to be a convection cycle that happens across this large living entity that we call "writers," where certain topics rise to the surface, and others fall below. This cycle of reading through and considering submissions was no different. One of the most urgent themes addressed in a number of pieces within this issue is that of bodily safety and security. This certainly resonated with me, as dread builds in our bodies with the disintegration of abortion protections, shootings in some of our safest spaces, and the incursion of anti-trans and anti-LGBTQ legislation across a myriad of states, counties, and municipalities in the U.S. Some pieces grappled with this loss of security, even within the walls of one's own home, as in Hiram Perez's gut-punching "John Travolta vs Farrah Fawcett" and Antony Fangary's potent poem "Khouf." Others found solace in the allyship and allegiance of family, as in Rachel Deutsch's "Another Place" and Jose Hernandez Diaz's "Abuelita's Prayers."

Within Issue #29, I also found a resounding swell of works claiming agency and expansive notions of identity in a world exceedingly bent on boxing people in. K-Ming Chang's "Mainlanders" points a mirror at the common xenophobic tropes of "us vs. them," while Timothy Nolan's "You Don't Say" wrests names from abusers and returns them to the next generation, in the hopes that they will no longer be used as cudgels by which to bully. "The Spring Business Brought About" by Isaac George Lauritsen contemplates the self in a world of influencers, brands, and corporations, while Rémy Ngamije's "We Bury Our Dead So White People Have Things to Discover" forces colonizers to capitulate to the demands of the ancestors of the cultures and countries from which they have pillaged.

Of course, the *Fourteen Hills* team had its hand in guiding some of the subjects that this issue explores by way of our special feature, which invited writers to submit flash creative nonfiction that in someway addressed the notion of "____ PUNK." The blank being, of course, anything and everything someone could envision "punk" encompassing. We received a number of exciting submissions that trace their way through Dayton, Austin, and San Francisco, and introduce the reader to dreamy skaters, scary gutter punks, and girls howling in the front rows of shows.

Regardless of subject, or theme, or tone, what all the pieces in Issue #29 have in common is vitality. Urgency. A rawness that I, as Editor-in-Chief, found refreshing and exciting. These pieces talk to each other along invisible filaments, provide scaffolding to the larger conversations occurring outside of pages and classrooms and Twitter discourse. Issue #29 is present and unapologetic. It is pointed and prophetic. It is loaded with language that had us leaping out of our seats with enthusiasm, so we recommend you read it somewhere soft and safe in case you, too, feel moved to move.

Quinn Rennerfeldt Fairchild
Editor-in-Chief, *Fourteen Hills*

MARCH 21, 2023

Fourteen Hills

THE SAN FRANCISCO STATE UNIVERSITY REVIEW

LANUGO

Bronte Lim

A RUSH OF COOL AIR mists over your naked form. The breeze travels from the open window to the crack beneath the bedroom door, and with it, tiny hairs whisper against your skin. The sun has yet to break on your east-facing window, towards which you sleep each night like a vine seeking light. Outside, an elderly woman is singing in the shrill, wavering style of mournful Chinese love songs. The tune tugs at a forgotten memory. *A woman... a man... love... rises the sun...*

Though your window faces another high-rise, its many windows like the facets of a compound eye, you do not worry about being seen. In the summer, a few reaching trees offer their leaves for modesty's sake, but near year-round, your bare, nocturnal flesh illuminates the lonely apartment. Regardless of whether trees bear crinkled leaves, few, or none. The local residents are old. Their prying eyes no longer feel human. They are inert masses, whorls of color and texture, needing maintenance. In your work, you know this well.

You rise. The decision follows the action, so familiar are you with the routine.

Poorly ventilated, the cupboard-sized room weeps from its walls, still wet from your post-work shower hours earlier. You gaze at your reflection, then pick up the name tag next to the sink. LINA TSE. You hold it up against your left breast and looked to the streaked mirror. Pale-skinned, black-haired stranger, skin dashed with soft hairs. The blankness of her gaze disturbs you and you turn away, dropping the nametag which clatters on the tile.

Into the shower now. The metal handle jams. Both hands, you wrench the handle once, twice, thrice—the water sputters. The hairs rise, lifted by goose-bumps springing to meet the chill. You reach for the razor with clinical calm.

In the daytime, you scrub old leather, a daytime routine as rote as the night's. At seven a.m., you rouse yourself from bed and exit your apartment building to the noisy embrace of Chinatown and walk ten minutes to the nursing home.

Vendors announce their goods. Herbal medicine shop windows open like pungent blooming flowers. The door to a plain brick building swings open at the press of a button, you flash your ID at the guard, and hang your coat in the staff lounge. Scrubs on, lanyard clipped, you begin your circuits through the activity room, the meal room, the private rooms.

Most residents are the parents and grandparents of immigrants who think in English and keep their Chinese names unused, an unwanted inheritance. A miserable few are elderly and alone, never-married or already-widowed laborers whose steps grew weak on a foreign shore. They speak in cusses, and come visiting hours, disappear into the back rooms. No matter—your job is to maintain their failing bodies, refurbish what can never be restored.

Work is a quiet time for you, but there is one co-worker, Leola, whose presence assaults your silence. She is beautiful like your sister, and talks to pass the time. Wheeling the residents in futile loops from room to room, she asks about their children, about their backs, and tells them about the news back in China. They are always keen to hear about the old place. *There is a new high-speed train being built. Shandong has a lot of rain this summer. Did you know, there are more and more Chinese people immigrating here? It is not lonely here at all anymore.* She looks right at them too, directly at the sunken blacks of their eyes.

Leola is a strange one, half Italian and half Chinese, having grown up in a small town far from the city, where her looks would have been gawked at, endearing or disturbing. Her Chinese surname chimes after her given name, misplaced. Her delicate, feminine flesh contrasts an inner yang aura, her bones emitting warmth. If you could, you would reach in between her arm bones and pull one straight out to examine, freed from its tender muscle and sinew. Leola has been working at Golden Life Assisted Living for nine years, many years longer than you have. Her beauty has not faded at all. To make matters worse, she considers you to be her friend.

A month ago, you found yourself alone with Leola in the kitchen. Most days, you timed your lunches to be eaten alone. A massive pot of clumpy rice gruel burped slow-bursting bubbles, cooling so that it could be spooned into gaping mouths. Leola's black hair, naturally wavy, was pinned back behind a clip topped with strings of woven, metal beads. She'd lost track of time rearranging a resident's family photos, she chattered. She described a private room tenant, the half-paralyzed Mr. Lam, who clucked his tongue to convey disdain until everything was arranged just right. You watched her pull a heavy glass lunchbox from the communal fridge and place it into the microwave. Suddenly, Leola clapped her hands together, a delightful remembrance surfacing. Oh! I was visiting my parents this weekend, and when I was speaking to them about you, I realized our last names are the same! Chay and Tse, just different dialects. Amazing, Leola beamed at you. Maybe we're distant cousins! China's a big place, but who knows?

You forced a smile in her general direction. The microwave beeped. Your own lunch, still icy, beaded condensation that trickled down your arm. Your eyes skirted up and down her figure. You felt your own body grow heavier. Yes, perhaps we are. Then, you lied: I don't really know my family there either.

Leola sat at the lunch table, face expectant. You watched as the light in her eyes dimmed to confusion, unsure why you continued to stand. You were unsure too. Without thinking, you excused yourself, turned, and found cover in the staff restroom. You waited many moments for Leola's sound of eating to cease, her brief and uncertain goodbye, the closing of the staff door as she returned to her shift. You watched your lunch swirl its way down the drain. Elbows propped on the sink basin, you followed that old, comfortable routine, studying your own face and body like a hated and distant other.

Later that afternoon, water pooling out the door of one of the independent suites led the orderlies to discover a crumpled pile of person, all legs and arms and skin. A newer admit, her move-in had caused a ruckus when she demanded the three-windowed room on the ground floor, close to the garden and the crafts room, her move-in boxes heavy and varied with hoarded piles of magazines, children's artwork, and empty margarine tubs filled with buttons and shoelaces. She was under your supervision, but consumed by the conversation with Leola, you had missed your afternoon rounds.

You assisted the orderlies in gathering her body, sweeping its loose and willowy appendages back towards its once-drumming torso. Her body was bare except for a gold chain around her neck, a pendant bearing the image of a chrysanthemum. Her hair, surprisingly black, sprung thinly from her pale scalp. When you squatted to help lift the body, you saw that the webs of skin on her bones were surprisingly smooth, the creeping green veins flush. The family arrived before the ambulance. Their wails were interspersed with a litany of memories.

It's not your fault. Leola's voice, her hand on your shoulder, made you jump. You finished your shift in silence, felt nothing as you trudged home and only tasted salt run down your cheeks in the slim shower stall, the din of water drowning out everything.

But that night, you awoke before the sun. Your mind felt unusually clear. A thin stream of clouds splayed across the dark sky, and a breeze kissed your collarbones. Your body felt soft, softer than it ever had before, your fingers tracing your skin in the dark for what felt like hours before you looked and saw the hair.

You reach for the razor, which sits in a puddle on an empty soap shelf. A spot of rust creeps down its side and leaks onto the porcelain. Drawing the razor up the length of your leg is a familiar, decade-long ritual. You hear your mother's disapproving voice. No idea where you got these from. Asian women aren't hairy, you've been told. They are sleek, feminine to an extreme. With the water still running, you lather your legs. They smooth quickly. It is a small adjustment to draw the razor up the full-length of your legs. You slow as the razor approaches the thick tangles of hair between your legs, careful around the mottled and dimpled curves of your thighs. The hairs slide down entrenched in foam to clog the drain, which chokes and gasps and spits back dirty water. Now the arms.

These are what he liked most back when you were thin. The caverns of your collarbones, the aching absence of flesh on the bones of your upper arm. He would grasp both your tiny wrists with a single hand and raise them to the early morning light, as though to see through them, then bring them to his mouth playfully, feigning a large and aggressive bite.

You were in nursing school when you met him. He approached you in a cafe where you studied alone, surrounded by papers and a tepid black coffee. He sat down at your table and introduced himself. He was older, not a student, but an adult working in the area. His chin stubbled, eyes self-assured. He bought you dinner that same night—a house salad, no dressing—and nodded while you babbled nervously about yourself, brought you to his apartment mere hours later.

Liqiu? He said. He could not pronounce the 'q' as a '*q*,' and said something more like Lee Koo. He leaned in, shrinking the already-small space between your bodies on the loveseat. You became breathless when he said, What a beautiful name. His warm arm blanketed your shoulders and your body melted into him; soon, you felt you could have followed him anywhere. A stray eyelash fluttered from his cheek. He was a wish incarnate. You preferred your English name, you murmured, Lina. He smiled, pressed his lips to your ear softly, and promised he would only call you Lee Koo in private.

Most nights, he called you his baby. He pushed inside your skin once, sometimes twice a night. He stayed over often in your lonely single room. You lived on campus, having told your parents that it would enable you to study harder, nixing the hour-long commute on the bus. After that first night, he insisted on coming to your room, a tiny single in a hallway of other anonymous rooms. The other girls began to whisper when you passed them, but you paid no attention to them. This was good. You finally had the intimacy all your friends had discovered so much earlier—a man who wanted to be inside you, who could find pleasure in your flesh. Your grades shocked you that semester. You told your parents that this was normal. The program had simply gotten more difficult.

Some nights, he would hold you tight against his flushed chest and stroke your long black hair, the tangled waves snagging his fingers. Good, good, he'd murmur. So good. The way his arm wrapped neatly around your waist, arching your back and pressing your breasts to him made you feel almost feminine, contoured against him, your body a complement to his. And he would fall asleep with you bent in that unnatural position, and you would lay there and watch his sleeping face at an angle too steep so that his chin was enormous and his brow scant. He breathed steadily, eyelids twitching through the landscapes of his dreams like a child.

Shaving your belly is harder. Bloated, it sits at odds with your hips creating awkward lines neither feminine nor masculine. Its center is fleshy, your belly button like a deep, caved-in sore. An angry reminder of your body's early excision from its mother. By the construction of its bones or muscle or tendons, your body makes a flat stomach impossible, though you had tried many times to discipline it into flatness. The uneven terrain causes you to nick yourself, and you wince, but purse your lips to remain silent.

As the hair clears and water runs down your bare skin, you peek past the shower curtain. Steam blurs your reflection. You think to when you were thirteen and angry, forced to live a summer with your grandparents in rural China. It was an ironic stay. Your father is a runaway, absentee son fleeing first to Shanghai, then Hong Kong, and finally to America. Perhaps that is where your penchant to flee originated. Father's parents were small and old, their withered features unfamiliar in a foreign home. They spoke to you in a dialect that sounded familiar and yet unintelligible, as though calling upon an alien part of your brain. Victoria, your little sister, would chatter back, somehow fluent, somehow always amiable, while you chose instead to nod for dinner, wave hello, smile and nod at any direct comment.

That summer you began cutting down food—eating first a bowl of rice, then half, then a mouthful. *Yi kou fan* became your most fluent Chinese phrase: *one mouthful of rice. A bit of rice.* It seemed promising that the character for mouth, *kou*, was an empty box. 口. You imagined yourself empty, like the monks of old who journeyed to places far from civilization, depriving themselves of food and water for spiritual enlightenment. You recall reading about Japanese Buddhists who would mummify their bodies alive, fasting in sealed underground chambers, the candles burning steadily as the flesh dissolved from their bodies.

Longer fasts, smaller bites. That summer you began doing sit-ups on the hard wood base of your bed until your stomach roared in protest at the slightest movement. You began coating your thighs in lotion and binding them in Saran Wrap while you slept, coaxing them to be slender, pleading away the faint puckered lines of cellulite.

You move from the bathroom to your bed, lying down half-covered, half-awake. The memories continue. That summer, Victoria shared a room with you. You moved a wall of chairs between your beds and hung a makeshift partition of an old sheet embroidered with red peonies, desperate to hide your shameful habits from her. Two years your junior, it was already obvious that she was growing to be a beauty. Victoria had the petite and delicate frame of your mother, your father's countryside pedigree visible only in a slightly broader nose and wider set eyes, but the imperfections were endearing. And she was shooting up too, taller than you already.

You ensured that before she came up to sleep, you and your wrapped legs were already hidden under a lumpy blanket. You awoke before her too, drenched in sweat, peeling off the wrap, your throat desiccated, your muscles aching, head pounding with the screeches of cicadas outside. The faint breeze from the mosquito-netted window peeled the scent of dried sweat from your sheets. While Victoria went to feed the chickens, or into the village square with your grandparents to purchase vegetables and fatty pork, you lay in bed listening to the same album of songs again and again, your legs exposed and gasping for air.

You shed energy. Your face perpetually pale, your hands cold even on the warmest of days. Long strands of hair, steaming with sweat, knotted in thick tendrils, loosened easily from your scalp. A ponytail was a limp dead animal in your hands. You asked your grandma to cut it short for you, and she did, in the kitchen with a pair of rusty scissor blades. You watched as though at a distance from your own body as the black locks dropped to the floor. With each dropping lock, you felt yourself moving farther away from your body. When she was done, your hair just below your ears, and your still face so round and pale, you scarcely recognized it.

You stayed in that distant place. In it, it was easy to move your body, observe it. It was only when Victoria suggested you both go swimming that you saw the full reality of your body, and hers. As you plunged into the water, feeling every last fold of your form drown in the warm water of the lake, you wondered if there was any reason to resurface.

So, you ate. You shoved bowl after bowl of rice and braised pork belly and greasy *meigan cai* down your throat, chunks of glistening fat flying onto the tabletop and grains of rice working into your sweaty hair. You could scarcely taste the rich meat, and the sensation of fat, the dark vegetables bursting with greasy, salty sauce, that was, after six weeks of restriction, overwhelmingly, *mockingly*, delicious. You ate until you nearly cried that night, begging for seconds, thirds, fourths, drinking the layers of soy sauce and fat drippings that pooled in the bottom of your bowl. Then sweets, thick, sticky pastries made with rice flour, white sugar, and soft red beans stewed into a rich paste with lard and rock sugar; you ate them without more than a few obligatory chews, crushing them flat with your molars and letting them slide down your throat.

The next three days, you were sick, violently. It was then that you dropped your first five pounds, the first bit of weight you ever lost. You burst into a radiant smile when you saw the number on the scale.

• • •

YOU SLOWLY SIT UP and let the towel fall away to the floor. The steam from the shower is thick, filling your sinuses. The hair shaved leaves fine points from countless follicles, and you stroke them like tender, lovable things, private yearnings for sun, yours to cherish and prune. Your toes play with the cardboard box beneath the bedframe, filled with notes from years of schooling. You thread a foot under the lip of the box and pull it out. It is labeled neatly with your name in capital letters. The flash cards are grouped in rubber bands, meticulously color-coded.

In the first year at nursing school, you had studied the developing fetus. You learned of the thin coating of hair that covers the body in abundance by the second trimester. The fetus, swelling with new tissues, sprouts hairs. You imagined a soft yellow body, tender as a summer-warmed peach, and thickly swathed in down, its tiny hands clasped tightly around an invisible something. While studying, you wrote the word onto one of a stack of dull mustard flash cards to study on the bus. It is the only word you remember now, the only word from a module that sits at the opposite end of human life from where your occupation brings you now.

Lanugo: a layer of hair that covers a fetus, first appearing at 16 weeks and present in abundance by 20 weeks.

You thought the image cozy. Lovely. Folded in a mother's womb, buoyed in fluid, and then in its own soft nest. Babies born prematurely often appear with traces of lanugo still on them. You had been delivered at 24 weeks, weighing 1.3 pounds, barely the size of a child's fist. Your mother spoke of it rarely, the emergency C-section a quiet knowledge mentioned to you by your father, a moment your mother refuses to discuss for its bad luck, but you imagine her cupping your infant body in her hands. Her first child. Soft and warm, small and tender, golden with down and swollen with new milk.

You know this could not have happened. You know you would have been in a plexiglass box among many, each holding a premature infant, hooked up to drips and wires and fed around the clock through an IV. Every function monitored. Every moment scrutinized for growth.

You were chubby in your first photo at home, a mass of soft folds like rising dough set atop a silk bedspread. You seem to smile but the curve of your mouth is indistinct in the largeness of your cheeks. Your mother had put on forty pounds in her short pregnancy. You were given rice porridge thick with sesame oil as your first food. By your first New Year's, you were swollen with so many folds that they permanently creased your skin, lines that criss-cross and tag a history of flesh. You thumb through the flash cards, scatter a few lazily across your bedspread before folding your body back beneath the sheets.

Your room is lighter now. Perhaps the sun is beginning to rise.

YOU WERE SURPRISED when he accepted the invitation to brunch. He had refused to meet your friends, your relationship primarily one of late-night encounters and daydreaming of his tender gaze. He was the first man to call you beautiful; his words were like lacquer, honeyed and redolent with hopes for forever. You felt small in his arms.

It's just my sister, you had said to him. Victoria's requests are fluff. You paused, elaborated at his silence. Meaningless.

He smiled and rubbed his stubbled chin against the top of your head, nestled you deeper in the crook of his shoulder. I'd love to meet her.

This moment plays through your head often. You wonder if the signs of infidelity were present then, or emerged later on. You wonder at love's blindness and cruelty. The memory bleeds quickly into the next, of a meal over dim sum with Victoria and a girlfriend of hers. You felt troubled by the attention he paid your sister, and the light-hearted manner with which she threw back her head to laugh. You busied yourself by counting and slowing your breaths until they melted into the noise of bustling carts of dumplings and buns, chewing through two plates of steamed vegetables, the dark sauce carefully dabbed off with a napkin. You mentioned the beginnings of your job hunt, your certification a few short credits away. You thought you saw him touch Victoria's thigh, an image that became more and more distorted with time, until you became convinced, though unable to voice, the belief that they had contrived to begin a relationship long before that meal.

Laying down, you relive it again and again. His hand on her thigh. His hand clasping your wrists. You imagine your hatred like the unexpected, sharp hardness of a peach pit. You imagine pressing it into a precise point of jaggedness between your thumb and forefinger, pressing it to your belly, collapsing it within yourself, deep, deep under layers of fat and viscera, to a place where no one would ever touch it.

A MAN... a woman...

Sunlight pries your eyelids apart. You must have fallen asleep atop the comforter, and now your skin is covered in goose pimples. The shrill voice continues to sing. You pick up your phone—6:57. Three minutes before your alarm. It is another Monday, another shift at Golden Life, spooning mush and moving bodies. Outside, the noise of early rush hour through Chinatown's narrow streets roars to life.

Victoria texted you. At 4:32 a.m., moments after you had likely fallen back asleep. Or had you woken up at all? The flash cards are gone; but then, perhaps you never scattered them. The harder you think, the faster the memories evaporate.

Call.

Call now.

Another time stamp. 4:54 a.m. She must have paused, to collect herself, to panic and text another confidante. Perhaps to wonder if you were really the person to contact.

I'm pregnant.

The messages continue, a deluge of one-line, two- to three-word texts, her sharp mind made erratic by distress. You let your phone slide out of your hand and lay still, flat on your back. Victoria, beautiful, slender Victoria. Pregnant. The words are like antonyms. But you remind yourself that no, she too is now a woman.

A man... a woman... your alarm blares.

You touch your arms, then your knees, curling into a fetal position. You let yourself sink into the memories of refeeding, the collapse after he left you. The six weeks in the ward as nurses ensured you chewed and swallowed every fattening morsel, the weeks that padded your form with soft flesh and used talk to coax out and clean the contusions of your mind. The door is so close and you try to imagine yourself rising. The alarm continues to blare. If you stand now, you can make it. But to where? You feel the seed within you germinating, the fine hairs on its twisting vines reach for the light, creeping towards the air blowing through your open window. Your skin is smooth but already you can feel the hairs returning, that long-studied promise of newness. Weariness returns, and you close your eyes to squeeze out every last trace of the sun, letting your flesh and hair seek it instead. You know not whether flowers or thorns or both will burst from your tired skin. You wait to be renewed.

HOW TO BUILD AN ACEQUIA

Mary Cisper

Each day the peaks lose more snow,
plum tree in blossom,

what you thought to call it: *the house*,

your rented apartments
filled with furniture and obituaries

like the Burgess Shale...

where did those creatures go?
could they have settled

deep in the Marianas:

gravity, sieving silt,
the absolute floor,

an exhalation,

the long return, the zones,
centigrades of withering,

populations, pelagic,

sunlight, everything craves,
you lift your face,

a dozen contrails backdrop

the knave of blossom,
one of the branches,

where does this one go?

brow-tapping to leap the subjective,
Venus belt at sunset,

the moon you mapped once,

in the room of the specific
you're looking for the door

of the general, perhaps

a feed bag in a stable,
perhaps a library,

when you search the screen,

notice the shadows
branches make, *X*s mostly,

saying unbearable fortune,

"meaning, the burden"
without placing all your

heavens in the casket,

or do you mean birdsong breaks in
on the unmade bed,

grandmother visits in a dream,

bank collapse or
oxbow, earnest money,

waterfall, in so many words,

in this ritual
will reach,

if I address the stream first,

sorting all else into heaps
until flowing becomes a way

of enfolding you.

HYMENOPTERA

Lauren Osborn

There's a tent at the edge of the local state fair between the sweet-sick, swirling lights of the tilt-a-whirl and a lone, sad petting zoo pony tied to a pole. Taped against its white canvas is a handwritten sign. Freak show. Tonight. 7 p.m.

The tent doesn't house the familiar horrors of childhood you remember—the two-headed calf, vivisected for voyeuristic feast, or the less shocking black tuft of chin hair against the cherried lips of a bearded lady. Instead, on the wooden stage is a small, normal-looking woman. She's in her early thirties, plainly dressed in a smart gray blouse and practical heels as if she were on her way to a blind date. Her black hair is snatched in a loose bun. At first, you think she's a guest who has gotten lost and wandered into the spotlight. At any moment she'll turn, embarrassed, and rejoin her place amongst the small crowd of bored teenagers and candy-stickied children. But she stands, black eyes unfocused over the heads of onlookers. At her side is a glass jar vibrating with a honeybee.

The lights soften into shadow. A child squeals and is shushed by their parent. The woman on stage offers the child an apologetic smile. You imagine how she looks to the bee, filtered through the glass, through compound eyes, a woman turned monster through perspective. She unscrews the lid and pinches the bee gently between finger and thumb, as if holding an expensive thread of silk. She offers the audience a clear view of the captured bee writhing between her fingertips, its muffled hum like a distant buzzsaw. Slowly, she presses the bee to her left forearm. The audience gasps as the stinger plunges into flesh. You watch for her reaction, expecting a grimace of pain, or maybe tears, but her face is stone. She releases her fingers from the insect's abdomen. It flies upwards, eviscerating itself and leaving the stinger behind. It'll die soon, alone in the dust, legs curled in an empty clutch. You wonder if anyone will find it when it does.

She walks through the crowd and showcases the wound. The venom sac still pumping its poison into her arm, slightly swollen into a small red cherry. You're not sure whether to clap. After all, you've been stung many times while plucking weeds from your garden, mowing the lawn. No one ever clapped for you. She bows before exiting behind the curtain and you wonder how much she gets paid—or doesn't—for this display of discomfort. The lights rekindle and once again everything is hollow, brought back from the brink of whatever magic lies in shadow. The teenagers blink away the bright, already forgetting what they saw and brag about how many times they can ride the tilt-a-whirl before they puke. The parents mumble about bedtimes. The children are begging for more.

You find yourself there again the following night. Perhaps pulled by curiosity. Or boredom. The pony outside has been retired and replaced by a fat pig rooting at the ground, trying to upheave the pole it's tied to. You expect a crowd but it's only you and two elderly women sitting front row. She is there too, barefoot, wearing a white-cotton dress. Her hair is loose and wrapped around her shoulders. You want her to notice, to remember you, her regular admirer, but she doesn't. She looks past blinking halogen bulbs and candy apple stands. Sharing the stage is a larger jar, painted black. But on second glance, the black squirms against the glass. Ants. A memory comes to you, your own encounter with an ant hill: the pus-filled knots rashed your ankles for weeks. But you don't leave. You can't. The lights dim. The show begins.

She loosens the jar's lid and balances gracefully on one foot, dipping her left toe into the ants. She might have been a ballerina previously, or maybe an acrobat. Her calves are hard carved and delicate. The ants swarm upwards in a dark shadow. A few escape across stage, towards the elderly ladies who swat them away with quick hands. The woman releases a small sigh—or was it a moan? Her leg is completely covered in a black mass. She scoops them upwards, across her arms, into her dress. Under it. In a moment, the atmosphere coils. You feel uneasy, as if you're trespassing. The elderly women shift in their seats. She smiles, puts an ant covered finger between her lips and licks. Something about her has changed after all. Or perhaps you never looked enough to begin with. She is hardened, composed of bone and angles. If she peeled away her flesh, you wouldn't be surprised to find shell. Her skin gooses with pin-prick stings. She folds into a bow. The show is over.

Months afterwards, you can't shake her from your head—her body speckled and stung. You want to chase after her that night, to witness the morbid aftermath. But you don't. You exit the tent, back into the world, now a little less familiar. Less safe. You purchase a skein of cotton candy from a stand, focusing on the way it melts against your tongue. A sweet nothing. Perhaps it was a party trick after all. Perhaps she wasn't actually allowing herself to be immolated by ants. Perhaps the bearded lady's beard was relocated pubic hair pasted with glue, the two-headed calf sewn together by a farmer hoping for a little extra cash. Despite wishing all your life for magic, you're numbed by the world's dishonesty. The cotton candy stickies your fingers and you consider sacrificing your hand into an ant bed, wondering how it might sting.

The following year, you sit front row. You've planned for this night, imagined it from every angle. She has haunted every ant bed in your backyard. Every fly tangled in web. At last, you're feet away, close enough to smell the salt and sharp sour of her skin. Her arms and legs are covered in a long black dress, as if in Victorian mourning. You imagine the map of whelps underneath that punctuate her thin body. You don't notice if there are others in the tent with you. Tonight, it's just you and her and the velvet box clutched in her left palm. You watch her large eyes, the twitch of her limbs. How many stings has she endured? How many hundreds have relished her suffering? You are no different. You yearn for pain.

She opens the box in a strange, slow proposal. You catch the exhale escaping from your lungs. A tarantula hawk, glossed black armor and half the size of her palm, rests against the silk lining. You flinch, anticipate the attack. The insect acts tame, crawls onto her hand, as familiar as a pet. Its red wings cut against the air. Their sound begs for violence. Will it sting her wrist? The soft crook of her elbow? Which would hurt more? The suspense gathers, fills the room hot and thick. You blink and nearly miss the swift movement of her hand to mouth. She swallows. The wasp, vanished.

This time, you follow after the bow, the applause, the blinding bright of lights rekindled. She's disappeared quicker than you can follow. You expect backstage swarmed with sword swallowers and red sequined jugglers; acrobats twisted in tight spaces. An empty dressing room is all you find. In the corner, a chest spills fabrics across the room. A vanity is haloed by dim bulbs. Amongst the clutter of plum lipsticks and violent rouges are jars filled with stinging things—velvet ants and cicada killers. Hornets and carpenter bees. Some are unknown and yet to be named. The room crackles with the sound of hard bodies beating against glass. The air crawls.

The silk-lined box lies open on the floor and on the mirror waits the tarantula hawk, black-bodied and ridged, seeking something soft to plunge herself into. You recognize her by the cut of calf, the sawing buzz inside your chest.

You open your mouth. You wait for her sting.

MANTODEA

Lauren Osborn

BECAUSE HE WANTS HER, he ignores the gleaming galea of her mandibles, the twitching antennae that run long and smooth down his spine as he tastes her spring-green flesh. Her insect brain knows no affection nor tenderness. No fickle feelings. Only hunger. Only sex. *Man and mantis can't mate*, people say, *it's unnatural*. But because he wants her, he hides no shame in the autumn-soaked fields of her home, golden grass gilding her wings, crowning her coxae. They are not the first lovers to invent taboo. They won't be the last.

He puts his ear to her chest, hears no quiet pulsing of a beating heart—only a faint hum of milky blood flowing through internal tubes—oxygen supplied as if by machine, not biological wonder. She coaxes him to her bed with clicks and clacks, rubbing her abdomen to signal she's ready. His human tongue feels clumsy in comparison with words that tumble deaf from his blood-thicked lips. What he wants to say is *you're the most beautiful thing I've ever seen*. What he wants to say is *I want you to have my brood*. Instead, he takes her abdomen between his palms, slips her iridescent wings beneath his fingertips.

It never occurred to him why a six-foot-tall mantis walked freely among us, what lab she might have escaped from, what harbinger of doom she signaled about our evolutionary ends. What occurs in that moment is the soft squeeze of her ovipositor, the ecstasy which escapes his human skin. He closes his eyes and imagines her eggs gathering smooth like grapes against a vine, hatching a magnificent marriage of human and insect, each with six arms and legs and fingers as sharp as tarsal claws. As the rapture racks between them, he doesn't register her mandibles around his skull—the muted crack of bone against palps. Rather, he feels his body spasm under the weight of her. He relishes in the release of male spite. He is fortunate to be spared the reflection of his death multiplied in her cold, compound eyes—the knowledge that she will soon nourish her eggs with what is left of him—the true meaning of *used*.

SANTA MUERTE AS HERSELF

Lauren Brazeal Garza

"Many seek my favor
        trying to purchase grace
by winding thin
        promises like scarves
                around my yellowed shoulders—
confusing me for other gods
whose illumination needs a source

                darkness is my resting state

dapple-hearted ones   loyal as crows
                accommodate the unction well
        not rushed with their assumptions
                                rattling prayers alone or in pairs
                their unstuck tongues fill rooms
with flowered words and bloodless palm-on-palm devotions

                they aren't misunderstood
I see them

        brave cigarettes' foul smoke to reach me
                                        begging for the imposition
                of hands before my bone-cool face at dusk

        I like them best
        on both knees this way and that

mouths wet
opened by their thirst
for a warm ear

I stroke the lace of their syllables and croon
dark songs from rose-smothered shrines

content to give instead of take

as water gives itself
to sate the drowning in their panic

it's always a mistake

when living things pretend
they can receive me in a way that matters"

GODMEN

Ronita Sinha

The year I turned twelve, I stepped into womanhood and Ma said I could technically become a mother. "Mahima, put this on." She held out a long shiny skirt, and I slipped into it. She looped my braids with ribbons so they resembled hollow ears on either side of my face, and together we walked to the temple for a blessing on my new-found nubility. The purohit, in between ringing a bell and lighting a cluster of incense sticks, extended his hand over my head and proclaimed, "May you have a hundred sons."

For me, however, far more terrifying things happened that year than that first flash of blood on my underpants.

A godman arrived in Prempur. I spotted him shuffling along the river on my way to the dance school. Just as no one knew where he came from, nobody could tell where he was going. He was tall, gaunt, and almost naked. The hairs on his bare chest were smeared with ash, and a saffron loin-cloth wound around his middle. I couldn't tell why, but this man scared me to no end.

On the heels of the godman, Khushi, with her nut-brown skin and dark unruly hair, moved to our town and became my best friend. Her father, a mining engineer, came to work for Python Copper, which in those days was the most coveted employer in Prempur.

Khushi was everything I was not. At twelve, she dreamt big dreams. She stood high on the victory stand on school sports day and walked away with prizes in science and English at year-end.

I, on the other hand, cherished the peace of the unambitious. All I wanted was to dance. She was the roaring ocean; I, a pond under shady trees. This girl, Khushi, I adored with all my heart.

Under the morning sun, the river of Prempur flowed like lemonade: serene, pristine. In the evening, the setting sun tipped its ripples with fire. The wind picked up our thoughts and carried them to the river where, like leaves fallen young from nearby trees, they eddied in its current. A banyan tree stood up from the riverbank, its base bound by a circular bench painted red that bled with the pounding of many monsoons. We sat on this bench with the tree as our shade, and in the ring of earth around its trunk, Khushi and I planted our dreams. We picked stones tumbled by the river in the color of our desires; burgundy shale for Khushi and for me, buttercream sandstone so brilliant I could see my eyes smiling in them.

One day, when Miss Bose read out Khushi's essay in class, delight pooled in her eyes, and the dimpled triangles at the two corners of her mouth tilted in a smile. After school, she took a tiny burgundy rock from her satchel and declared, "This is going under the banyan tree."

She ran ahead, I followed. Every time a dream was fulfilled or a dream born, we buried a colored rock around the banyan tree like trophies we gave ourselves. Then we sat and chatted with our third friend, the river.

"Thud, thud, thud." The godman beat his stick on the ground indicating for us to make room for him on the bench. His rusty hair hung in matted ropes and his beard, the color of sand, touched his belly. I inched closer to Khushi. He folded his legs under him and sat on the circular bench, behind me. I stole a look at him. A vermillion mark blazed on his forehead, its brilliance competing with the strange light that shone from his eyes. I didn't hear him utter a single word yet his lips buzzed all the time.

"He looks so holy," I whispered, afraid his holiness might crack like Ma's porcelain tea cups.

"Why are you whispering?" Khushi whispered back.

"Can't you see he's meditating?"

The godman must have moved up on the bench because I could feel the heat from his body. I sensed him gazing at the river through my braided hoop, his lips moving. I shunted closer to Khushi.

We kept up our conversation in low tones, our words rustling like leaves. Petal by petal, I unfurled a rosebud I had picked from our garden.

"But doesn't it all start with a dream?" Khushi said. The hair around her heart-shaped face lifted in the breeze, and the sun glinted off her gold ear stud.

"Sure," I said. "If I don't dream of being a dancer how can I ever become one?" The flame of Khushi's ambitions had begun to lick me. "I want to go to Calcutta and join a big dance school and train to be a dancer." Happiness leapt up the ladder of my ribs.

"Then let's go together, Mahima. I will study plants. Did you know the scientist Jagadish Bose said plants can feel pleasure and pain just like we do?"

"Really?" I slipped the half-opened rosebud into my skirt pocket.

We chatted awhile about the flame-out experiment we did in science class.

We each lit a candle over which we poured carbon dioxide to see how it snuffed out the flame. "All those tiny fires made Mrs. Roy a bit nervous, don't you think?" I laughed. In the rose-scented air, our giggles shivered across the wavelets. The ancient banyan tree above us sighed in silence. We did not notice when the godman slipped away.

He wandered from home to home and the women gave him food. Ma laid a mat for him on the marble floor of our veranda, and on a large glossy banana leaf, she served him a mound of rice scooped out at the top. She filled the hollow with thick slurpy daal in which floated chunks of vegetables. He leaned his staff against the wall while he ate. At the end of the staff hung a cloth bag bulging with mysterious possessions.

"He's a poor, homeless man. He has dedicated his life to God," Ma said, her fingers steepled in reverence at her forehead. And true to his godliness, he muttered a blessing on our home before he shuffled away leaning on his stick.

"What did he say, Ma?"

"He speaks in Sanskrit, the language of the wise and the holy, so I am not too sure."

"What does he stare at all the time?"

"He's a godman, a sadhu, and he is looking at God himself. You can tell from his eyes, he's in a trance."

KHUSHI HAD JOINED my dance school and we looked forward to our rehearsals. There was only a week left to the annual show and the practice sessions became rigorous and long-drawn. The ghungoors we wrapped around our ankles jingled in jute bags, slung over our shoulders, as we walked. We wore tights under our skirts so when we did the thirty-two chakkars, our underwear would not fall prey to the prying eyes of the drum-player. His gaze wandered but his smile stuck to his lips. Our skirts spread out straight like lotus leaves, quivering in the wind of our whirls.

We rehearsed in a large room with a dais, about a foot off the ground at the long end. Bishuda, the music director, sat cross-legged and straight-backed in one corner of the dais, his bluish-black hair brushed back to reveal an august forehead. His name was a household one and often heard on All India Radio. He had deigned to offer his music for such an amateur performance as ours only because his wife was the principal's old friend. The principal, eager to show her gratitude to Bishuda, instructed the students, "When you girls come in, make sure you fold your hands in a namaskar before Bishuda."

And Bishuda sat on the dais with a godlike aura as we offered our obeisance.

A batch of senior girls was practicing their routine. I sat below the dais on the shiny mosaiced floor, facing Bishuda. My chin rested on my forearms folded neatly along the edge of the dais. Eight ceramic bowls sat in a half-circle in front of Bishuda, graded in size from small to large in a complete octave. From a pitcher he poured water into each bowl, adjusting their levels every now and then, and running a light wooden mallet over the rims, like fingers over piano keys, testing the accuracy of each note. *Sa Re Ga Ma Pa Dha Ni Sa* trilled the bowls. If one did not ring true to his ear, he adjusted the water in it, either adding or ladling some back into the pitcher.

"Do you know what this is called?"

His deep voice startled me. The great man had spoken. And to me. Black-rimmed glasses framed a pair of gleaming eyes. If the godman's look was vague and faraway, Bishuda's was immediate and penetrating.

"N-n-no."

"It's called a Jal Taranga. Waves of Melody. Do you want to help me pour the water?" His smile cleaved my heart. His eyes smouldered like coal fires, deep and unwavering.

I was the chosen one. Trembling, I got on my knees by the dais and took the pitcher from him.

"Could you pour some in number six?"

Sixth from his side or mine? I was confused.

"Always count from smallest to largest."

I breathed again.

"Slowly, slowly, very slowly," he said. "Here, let me show you."

He reached over to my side and his left palm folded over my right hand on the pitcher handle, guiding me as I leaned in towards the bowls. The water dribbled thin as a string, at times invisible like thoughts. Bishuda's pitcher-holding knuckles brushed my chest. I didn't look at him. I couldn't have him think my focus was faltering. *Of course, it was an accident.* His palm trapping my hand was fleshy and moist. His knuckles scorched through my blouse, grazing up and down, up and down in deliberate mesmerizing motion, the pressure mounting. My heart hammered in my ears, dry and erratic. I shrank as far back as possible into my fear. The knuckles pushed harder and harder like a dinghy pressing against the gentle river-breeze. And, like the infinite ache in my young breast, the water drooled endless, from bowl to bowl to bowl.

"Girls, put on your ghungoors," screamed the dance teacher. Bishuda's hand slithered off mine. I wanted to wash his sweat off my hand but there was no time. Khushi already had her bells tied around her ankles. I bent down to tie mine, and the floor, cracked and buckled by my tears, splintered into countless pieces.

I was in an ocean, entombed in silence, the heaving, swaying water blocking my ears. A cluster of girls like colorful fish chattered in a corner, a shark with pointed teeth set in an arc, beat the hand drums, and a slimy eel stroked a mallet along a Jal Taranga. The music did not reach my ears. Someone was pulling my hand and from far, faraway Khushi's voice drifted towards me. Breaking a million bubbles, I surfaced.

"Mahima, what's wrong with you? Come on, it's our turn." Khushi pulled me into the circle of dancers in the center of the room. *Khushi means happiness and Mahima, glory. Why do parents name their children after things they cannot promise?*

My feet struck the ground, *Dha dhin dhin na. Dha dhin dhin...*

"I heard a misstep. Stop, stop!" Bishuda's voice boomed from the dais. "When will these girls ever learn to keep the tempo?"

Everyone halted and the dance teacher glared at me. "If you don't practice at home then stay home, don't come for the rehearsals, okay? Now go sit down."

My cheeks burning, I found a spot as far from the dais as possible.

"See, you can never fool the practiced ear of a musician like Bishuda," said the dance teacher, slipping a fawning glance at the music director.

THEN IT WAS OVER. Amidst a great fanfare of light and sound, the annual concert was over. Rehearsals gave way to regular classes and Bishuda departed. A voice insisted in my ear, *it was not an accident, it was not an accident*, and with a creeping certainty, I started to believe it. Guilt and shame coiled around my heart like a two-faced serpent. Bishuda had singled me out. I had no rhythm sense. I was to blame. He punished me. At night, shame soaked my pillow yet I could not find the words to share my despair with anyone, not even Khushi. Shamefully, I inhabited two friendships with her; one with no secrets and another, sullied by a terrible one.

The scorching summer yielded to a lush monsoon. A soppy green dripped from eaves and tree branches while women chased an ephemeral band of sunlight, from terrace to yard to balcony, to dry their laundry. The river of Prempur swelled, threatening to overflow and warning signs had to be posted along its bank.

I practiced hard at my dance and it bore fruit. On the last day of the term, I was awarded a certificate of merit. Khushi and I ran to look for a yellow sandstone piece, and I planted it under the banyan tree, covering it with the damp sticky dirt, my fingers quick and happy. A weight slipped from my chest and as we walked home, I thought of telling Khushi what Bishuda did to me that summer. *I was not a bad dancer after all.* As this thought swirled in my mind, Bishuda's action seemed more a transgression than a punishment. Before I could form the words, Khushi grasped my hand.

"Mahima, I have something to tell you."

"About Bishuda?"

"No, about the godman, the sadhu. He's not a good person, Mahima." Khushi's eyes were the embattled monsoon-river of Prempur.

Grey clouds like elephants loomed in the sky and the day trembled on the brink of premature dusk. We walked faster.

"Let's meet under the banyan tree tomorrow and I'll tell you everything. You need to know, Mahima, you need to know."

Lightning skidded across the sky, illuminating everything in a blaze of dazzling white. My breath was ragged, my words halting.

"Khushi, I too have something to tell you. During our dance rehearsals...." A growl of thunder drowned my words.

We started to run, parting ways near the post office as we always did. My house, close to the main road, came up first. Khushi lived further into the town, opposite the soccer field where local teams held matches. Beyond the field, a railway track wound its way, and train rumbles floated for miles in the calm midnight air. We waved to each other and in the luminous light of the clouded evening, Khushi's teeth flashed like a fistful of fireflies. She was gone and I, suddenly alone, continued homeward.

The smattering of people on the street looked bent on beating the brewing storm. A few cars whizzed by on the ribbon of asphalt, at the end of which I could see the river flowing black as tar. Panting. Heaving. Lusting.

I spotted the godman approaching from the opposite direction and Khushi's words rang in my ears. I edged sideways to make room for him on the narrow pavement. His gait was a canter and his eyes fixed at a point on the river as though he could see where it emptied into the Bay of Bengal. Something was different, instead of that trance-like stare his eyes blazed like coal fires, deep and unwavering. As he passed me, his thin sinewy arm shot out and grabbed my crotch in an instant of astounding pain. I screamed and sprang into a lamppost smashing my head. He broke into a run, an athletic, practiced run, and disappeared around the corner that Khushi had minutes ago.

I had to warn her. I took a few steps after him, the pain pulsating through my whole body from where he had clutched me. Something sticky dribbled from my temple into my eye and when I lifted my finger, it scraped away a smear of blood. My own terror then turned me around, and I found myself stumbling in the opposite direction, towards home.

I collapsed at the bottom of our veranda steps. Ma rushed to me, her face the colour of curdled milk.

All I could utter was, "Khushi, Khushi, Khushi," and, "godman, godman, godman," but the words came out so garbled that no one understood me until Ma finally made some sense of them.

Khushi had not reached home. Her mother assumed she had come home with me to wait out the storm. Ma put the phone back in its cradle and clung to me, kissing my wound which she had cleaned and dressed. Outside, the hot rain lashed around rattling the window panes.

I remained in delirium for two nights and two days, unable to sit up, eat or speak. Doctor Sen, our family physician, paid a house call. He said I was in shock and prescribed some tranquilizers and paracetamol to keep the fever in check.

I learned later, while I lay in bed disoriented and febrile, the fathers, brothers, and husbands of our small community mounted an enormous search for Khushi. They trampled through thickets, they scoured the river, they knocked on every door. They moved and moved like a town possessed as if even a moment's rest would be an insult to Khushi. Sliding down a moonbeam, she would berate them, "*I was right here and you couldn't find me? You didn't try hard enough.*"

The same day my fever broke, they found Khushi's body amidst the bracken along a narrow inlet of river, not far from the wagon shed by the rail tracks. Her father was summoned to identify the corpse.

It didn't take long for my parents to draw a connection between Khushi's killing and my bleeding temple. This time I cast aside the nauseous stirring of shame and told them the truth of that evening. What I kept from everyone was that tiny rock of guilt lodged in my heart. I failed Khushi by not running after the godman to yell a warning to her. I was on the main thoroughfare but Khushi had already started on a lonely stretch of the road where it would be hard for anyone to hear her screams. I could have alerted other people too. Instead, that evening, I picked the path of least resistance and ran home.

The news of Khushi's rape and murder coursed through Prempur like venom from a snakebite. Men, their eyes listless with defeat, hung in knots at the bazaar discussing how such evil could befall a decent town like ours. Anxious mothers clasped their children's hands whenever they stepped out, and no child was left alone to sit and dream under the banyan tree.

A WEEK LATER, I sat up in bed sipping some soup while Ma turned on the television. She paused on a channel airing marches, organized across the province, in protest against Khushi's incident. Throngs of angry men and women, their fists punching the air, filled the screen.

"Prominent intellectuals, thinkers, and musicians also joined the protests..." read the strident voice of the broadcaster, and just then the camera panned and focused on the face of Bishuda. A tremor shot through my body. Someone thrust a microphone into his chin, and for a heart-stopping moment, his gaze bore into me. Then looking boldly into the camera he delivered his statement. "We not only need stricter laws in this country to protect our women, especially our young girls but we need to teach our men to respect every woman out there.

Women, the mothers of our nation..." Ma clicked her tongue and snapped the television off.

My father, who was the corporate lawyer for Python Copper, wanted to litigate on behalf of Khushi's family pro bono but no defendant could be found. The godman was the prime suspect but he had vanished from Prempur leaving no trace. According to reports, investigators found a trail of vermillion on the lifeless skin of Khushi's neck.

At night, Khushi's sleepless parents sat on the bench with faded paint, where Khushi and I had dreamt our dreams. They stared out at the river littered with moons, their eyes hopeful, waiting for Khushi to rise from the water and sashay into their arms. They would gently push the tendrils of wet hair from her face, clasp her to their bosoms and take her home.

Khushi comes to me often in the fragrance of frangipani, in the tilting triangles of a smile, and in the giggle of ghungoors at girls' ankles.

No, I did not become a dancer. The sharp winds of chronic ennui whittled my dreams to a wisp. My subject is botany and, five years ago, seeking comfort in the unfamiliar, I emigrated to Canada. Now, at forty-two, I work for an herbal pharmaceutical company. The subway takes me to my office in downtown Toronto, but what brings me greatest joy and solace are assignments away from my desk. I wander in distant forests, studying plant life in all its baffling variety, searching for healing for a myriad of human ailments.

Neither did I have *even one* of the hundred sons the temple purohit blessed me with on the day I transitioned to a woman. I live alone in a flat by the lake, treasuring the steady, dependable companionship of solitude.

Before I left Prempur, I dug out the tiny rocks that Khushi and I planted under the banyan tree and walked down to the river. At the water's edge, I paused to listen to their rattle one last time within my cupped palms. Then, swinging my arms above my head, I flung the stones into the river. Each rock traced a different arc in the air before plunging into the water. I waited till the ripples died down and walked home alone.

THE SPRING BUSINESS BROUGHT ABOUT

Isaac George Lauritsen

I failed my sales endeavor.
In an effort to express love for friends
I put their teeth on t-shirts,

made a mix-tape of their laughter
but I couldn't hack it
in the capital world.

It put me in a winter
so I had to rebrand
my way back to life.

I thought to be a box
opened by slicing
my tape with a key.

I wanted a dog to hop out.
I wanted a kettle to whistle
like an annoyingly good mood.

I wanted nothing.
I wanted infinite contentment
to stretch forward

like this season's shawl
stemming from my
blood-pumping apparatus.

"Apologies for my unseasonal
color, my off-brand blood."
That's what the customer service center

of my throat would say.
All I have is this park
where families star

in the weather's movie
cast as proponents of
linen. I'm a walking advertisement

for the spring
who's busy patrolling
the geraniums in the shorts

she recently unpacked.
I don't look
at my portable computer

in case a coupon interrupts
with its numbers and sneakers.
I use my nose to observe

purple petals—
the scent the base ingredient
for made-up grapes

hanging from this tree
the great industrialists
have just released.

DREAM CATHEDRAL

S.A. Leger

Before Dream Cathedral, there were earthly things.
Birds with bills shaped for eating. Trees with leaves
shaped for worshipping the sun. Men shaped as canvases
where paint and light and the impact of rushing geysers spoke

in iambic pentameter—
        "I strip the feathers from crown to atlas,
        from bill take cry and orange gape. I steal
        back flight and perch and haunt; beneath the crop
        and gizzard. Wingless beast do not now fly
        nor rest your head upon your breast. Commit
        your life to oaken dark for my records."

For our records, there were numbers. Hall upon hall, etched
upon every tile, every stone, there were numbers.
Before Dream Cathedral there were signs of life. There were rings
in teeth, age marks in the otoliths of fish. There were men

counting in Fibonacci Sequence—
        come
        home
        to me
        beneath swarms
        of midnight locusts
        I wait, hour on hour, lunar glow.

Before, there were names. Now only Dream Cathedral
so named by the people who leave future items
in their wills. Properties, jewels from caves, collections
of fossilized plastic among petrified wood. Dream Cathedral
orbits the sun, a yellow snake of magma
shedding its fiery scales into the breath of patchy ozone.

Dream Cathedral is an epistolary for man as carbon—
    Dear future,
        Our neurons are sound.
        Legally, we have aged.
        We make this Last Will with charred sticks, our wishes
        influenced by truth, our duress, by heat.
        We are married to the preservation of our destiny.
        Though if you are reading this,
        we are no longer married.
        At the time of executing this Last Will,
        we have the following children:
        wisdom
        and bipedal motion.
        Though if you are reading this,
        we no longer have children.
        We appoint Dream Cathedral as executor.
        If Dream Cathedral predeceases us,
        we will come home
        beneath skies of electric light
        we will make fire once again
        we will mark our days by lunar glow.

BEHIND CLOSED DOORS #1

Christopher Rodriguez

pastel & charcoal on paper
12" × 12"

BEHIND CLOSED DOORS #2

Christopher Rodriguez

oil on canvas
36" × 48"

THE PINE BARRENS

Don Zancanella

GIRL DETECTIVE DAISY FROST and her creator, Luella Cosgrove, have switched places. Now Daisy will write the books and Luella will solve the crimes. But as Daisy takes her seat at the typewriter, she reminds herself that there is no actual Luella Cosgrove. Or rather there are many Luellas, all of them employees of Edward Stratemeyer's legendary book factory. When a new Daisy Frost mystery appears, it might have been written by Tillie Goldberg, Frank DeMarco, Lydia Robinette, or Inez Maddox—or by two of them working as a team. Therefore, Daisy is faced with a dilemma. If Luella Cosgrove is actually Tillie and Frank and Lydia and Inez, which one of them will take her place as the heroine of the novel? She picks Inez. Yes, Inez it shall be.

Since Daisy has been a girl detective for several years, she has a good sense of how to write the sort of adventure stories youngsters like to read. A valuable vase will go missing, red herrings will be cast about, and the solution will depend on Inez's ability to see the significance of a clue that has been in plain sight since chapter one.

Before she starts writing, Daisy reviews the rules—Mr. Stratemeyer's rules—governing the Daisy Frost series, as well as others like it, including the Hardy Boys, the Happy Hollisters, and the Dana Girls.

1. There can be nothing physical between male and female characters. Not even implied.
2. Every chapter must end with a cliffhanger. (She recalls a time she was involved in an actual cliffhanger. It was in *The Case of the Yellow Convertible*. How terrifying it was to cling to a ledge with her fingertips high above a rocky gorge.)
3. Characters may not change or marry. (This is obviously related to

#1 but she's not sure about the word "change." Is it not true that character change is one of the engines that drives fiction? Is it not true that at the end of the story she, or in this instance Inez, will inevitably know more than she did at the start?) Then again, when the next book in the series commences, everything will be as it was before.

4. Good people have dogs, bad people have cats. (This one is ridiculous. She may have to have a word with Mr. Stratemeyer about it.)
5. There should be no drunkenness or taking of dope. (Well of course. Why even bother putting that on the list.)

Although some of the rules seem less important than others, Daisy does not expect to have any difficulty following them. After all these years they are in her blood, part of her very being.

Still, she is a bit concerned about her heroine. Inez is bookish, shy, lives with two girlfriends in a cold-water flat beside the elevated train tracks, and recently turned twenty-six. Can she play someone ten years younger than herself? She does have the face for it—the skin of a twelve-year-old and eyes of china blue. But there's more to it than appearance. Inez seems a bit world-weary, as though in her mind, in her vision of herself, she's already crossed into middle age. She lacks the optimism a girl detective ought to have. When Inez Maddox gets up in the morning she thinks, *Why is it that every day seems exactly like the one before it* instead of *There's no telling what excitement the future holds.*

On the other hand, this is a book, not real life, and Daisy is the author. Inez can be her puppet. She can make her think and do whatever she pleases. To get things started, she changes her hair. Instead of mouse-brown it will be blonde and curly, like the hair of Glenda Farrell in the series of movies about Torchy Blane, female reporter. That alone causes Inez to seem more youthful, more energetic, and even sexier although not so sexy as to violate any rules.

At the end of her first day as a writer, Daisy covers her typewriter, leaves the office, and goes home to her father, lawyer Mason Frost and their housekeeper, Hazel Fischer. Daisy is relieved to see that changing places with Luella Cosgrove (or rather Inez) doesn't mean she has to go home to a cold-water flat beside the tracks. She is still a vivacious teenager (she checks herself in the mirror to be sure), still lives in a large house in a leafy neighborhood, and still has a closet filled with clothes for every occasion (but again, she checks to be sure). Supper is an hour away so she lies down on her bed and thinks about Inez. She hopes she'll enjoy being a detective. Surely it will be better than writing, which Daisy can already tell is a bit of a grind. Maybe in this book she'll include a handsome boy and a hint of romance. Of course there can be nothing physical, not even innocent touching, not even implied.

The next morning she has breakfast with her father and takes the bus into the office. Although things are quiet when she first arrives, by midmorning the Stratemeyer Building is a hive of activity. One whole wing is devoted to the Hardy Boys and another just to thinking up new characters for new books. Daisy's desk is in an open area along with desks occupied by other writers of Daisy Frost mysteries. When all the typewriters are clacking it can sound like a passing train.

On her desk is what's called a synopsis. It's a general outline for the book she'll be writing, provided by someone upstairs. Someone very high up, although probably not as high as Mr. Stratemeyer himself. This one is titled "The Mystery of Wild Horse Canyon." As soon as she sees it, she thinks, "Oh goody, I'm going on a trip." But an instant later, she realizes it's Inez who will be going on a trip. While Daisy remains in this dingy office, hunched over her typewriter, churning out words, Inez will be in Nevada having a ball. She quickly shrugs off the disappointment. If there's one thing Daisy Frost is not, it's a complainer. Even during the most trying of times, her chin is up.

Daisy decides to begin by having Inez receive a letter from a cousin inviting her to spend two weeks on a ranch. Which cousin? It probably doesn't matter. In her experience cousins appear in books and disappear again like sparrows at bird feeders, seldom staying for long. She'll call this one Bill. In the letter, Bill says she'll get to ride horses, go camping in the desert, and learn to throw a rope. At this point Daisy pauses. Does one "throw" a rope or "cast" a rope? And should it be a lasso? Or perhaps a lariat? This writing business isn't easy. But then she remembers about editors. The editor will take care of it. She smiles and moves on.

She likes the idea of beginning the book with a letter and wonders if it's been done before. Suppose it's actually her own invention and Mr. Stratemeyer notices. How exciting that would be. She pictures a memo coming from his office: "Daisy Frost, who has recently joined our team, came up with the idea of starting a book with a letter. It's an ingenious technique and I encourage others to give it a try." She closes the letter with a line calculated to propel the reader forward: "'While you're out here maybe you can help us find our white stallion,' Bill says. 'We think someone stole it but we haven't any proof.'" Cliffhanger anyone?

She wonders briefly if she should call the heroine Inez not only in her own mind but in the book itself. Yet that wouldn't make any sense. After all, she's writing a Daisy Frost mystery. The character will have to be Daisy, as played by Inez. Then again, if the two of them are switching places, shouldn't she call herself Inez, at least while she's sitting at the typewriter? As she's pondering all this, Frank DeMarco, whose desk is across from hers, says, "Tell me, Daisy, do you remember the name of Daisy's high school English teacher? I know she was mentioned in *The Clue of the Broken Locket* but I've forgotten what it is."

Well, that answers her question. Frank just called her Daisy. So even if Inez will be playing the part of Daisy Frost in the upcoming book, she herself will remain Daisy Frost. It's complicated but also quite a relief. Writing a book is going to be difficult enough without pretending to be someone she's not. "Mrs. Wallace," she tells Frank and then gets back to work.

In the days that follow, Daisy immerses herself in the writing. She always arrives early and when the story is going well, leaves late. Outside, America is in the midst of a depression. People are homeless. They have no jobs and need food. Her family is one of the fortunate ones. She's getting paid to write Daisy Frost mysteries, her father's legal practice is thriving, and they have even been able to keep their housekeeper Hazel employed.

Her father often gets new clients because of her detective work and wouldn't like knowing she's changed jobs. To prevent him from becoming suspicious, she tells him she's working on a new case. Something about a gold amulet and mysterious footprints in the mud outside the Museum of Art. But to be honest, Daisy hasn't minded stepping out of the limelight. For one thing, she no longer feels the need to dress so perfectly. And when she speaks across the desk to Frank, she enjoys being able to curse: "Can't wait for the fucking weekend, Frank." "If the elevator operator closes the door in my face again, I'll kick his goddamn ass."

She wonders how well Inez is adapting to her new role. She's certainly obedient enough—when Daisy writes a scene for her, Inez moves through it like an automaton and flawlessly speaks every word. But Daisy continues to worry about the fact that Inez is twenty-six. Therefore, she decides to test Inez's ability to act her age.

It comes at the point in the book where Cousin Bill has taken Inez into town to look for clues. Recently, they have learned the white stallion is not the only horse that's been stolen. Others are missing from nearby ranches, suggesting a gang is doing the dirty work rather than a single thief. Inez goes into a saloon, stands at the bar, and orders a shot. She flirts with the bartender and asks if he's heard any loose talk. "About a horse," Inez says. "A big white one. Whoever has it will be trying to sell it for a high price."

The bartender studies her. He leans forward and narrows his eyes. "How old are you?"

"Old enough to know better."

"Don't get fresh with me, missy. I shouldn't have served you. And I don't know nothin' about no horse."

So the experiment is a success. Bartenders are notoriously astute judges of character. If he thinks the girl sitting at the bar is Daisy Frost, teenage detective, then Inez is doing her job. As for the drinking, that's a small matter that can be corrected in the next draft. Filled with confidence, Daisy writes an exciting chapter in which Daisy and Cousin Bill saddle up a couple of fillies and ride out into the slickrock canyons, hot on the trail of the gang of thieves, beneath a buttermilk moon. When it's complete she takes it to the copy editor. "This is a good one," she says.

A few days later, shortly after lunch, a woman from upstairs visits her desk. She says, "Mr. Stratemeyer loved your chapter."

Daisy looks up from the typewriter. "Oh, I'm so pleased. I'm doing my best."

"And he'd like your help."

"Of course," she says. Since she owes her very existence to Mr. Stratemeyer, she has no choice but to agree.

"It's about Inez Maddox. You've been working with her lately, is that right?"

"Yes. She's my..." Daisy's not sure what to call her. My protagonist? My heroine? My stunt double? "In the book I'm working on, she's playing the role of Daisy Frost."

"Maybe she was, but not anymore. She's gone missing. Since you know her so well, we'd like you to see if you can find her."

"Find Inez? I wouldn't know where to look. And I'm not sure my father will allow it."

"Why would he care? Frank will drive you." She motions to DeMarco who is busy typing. "We're counting on the two of you to locate her and bring her back."

"From Nevada?"

The woman looks puzzled.

"Nevada," Daisy says again. "*The Mystery of Wild Horse*—"

"Oh, no, it's all being done in New Jersey, a place called Hosford. Only a three-hour drive away."

Daisy is taken back a bit—Wild Horse Canyon in New Jersey? But it makes sense. In the books Daisy Frost lives in Apple Valley, Indiana, while Daisy herself lives in Queens. "Now I understand," she says. "Three hours. And Frank will drive. Yes, I think I can do that."

Before she departs for the day, she and Frank agree that he'll pick her up at home in the morning. With luck they'll go to New Jersey, find Inez, and then she can continue writing the book—although who will play Daisy Frost after Inez is brought back is something she'll have to figure out.

She asks Frank if he'll know where to go.

"Yeah, yeah, Hosford. It's a little burg down in the Pine Barrens. I been there lots of times. Nothing to worry about." The way he says it is unsettling—as if *Nothing to worry about* means *You're sticking your nose where it doesn't belong.*

That evening she tells her father she'll be going to New Jersey the next day.

"New Jersey? What sort of case are you working on?"

"Missing person. A writer friend is going to take me there. I'll be back in time for supper."

"Good luck on the case. Give Hazel a call if you're running late."

As she gets ready for bed, she feels herself becoming Daisy Frost again. Girl detective. Finder of missing persons. Maybe she'll bring Inez home and they'll change places again. Inez can write the rest of the book and she can go back to New Jersey—Wild Horse Canyon—and help Cousin Bill foil the outlaw gang's plot.

However, Frank DeMarco fails to show up. He said he'd be there at eight and he's already an hour late. She knows what happened. Frank has a drinking problem. Once or twice a week he doesn't get to the office until ten a.m. On those days, his eyes are bloodshot and he wears the same clothes as the day before. Mr. Stratemeyer puts up with it only because Frank is the fastest worker on staff. He wrote *The Secret of the Harvest Moon* in twenty-four hours, and it's one of the most popular books in the series. How well she can remember finding the letter covered with writing that looked like a secret code. Only when she held it up in the moonlight was she able to read the words. As long as Frank can come up with ideas like that, no one will care if he drinks.

She'd ask her father to drive her, but he's already gone into work. So there's only one solution. After locating the extra set of keys, she opens the garage door as quietly as possible (not wanting to alert Hazel) and backs out onto the street. She has her learner's permit and feels confident she can get herself to New Jersey and back. A block from the house she pulls over, finds a map in the glove box, and studies the route. Then off she goes.

It takes a great deal of concentration to steer a car and keep it at the proper speed. Especially on the highway. She had no idea it was so difficult. Until now she's only driven around the neighborhood with her father sitting beside her, telling her what to do: "Daisy, use your turn signal. Daisy, stay in your lane." The traffic today is terrible. Maybe it always is. But after she crosses the bridge into Jersey, she begins to relax. Except for one thing. She keeps seeing the same car, a maroon coupe, in her rearview mirror. Is it following her? And if it is, why?

Overcome with panic, she leaves the highway and goes right left right left and finally left again. Then she looks back. Phew, the coupe is gone. Rejoining her chosen route, she stomps on the gas and continues south. Many of the stores she passes are boarded up, and the houses need paint, have broken windows, or are exhibiting other evidence of disrepair. She's heard her father say their neighborhood hasn't suffered as much as most parts of the country and now she sees what he means. There's a long line of disheveled men waiting to get into a building. Is it a soup kitchen or are they hoping to apply for a job? Things seem worse with every mile. Under some trees, a cluster of canvas tents. In a vacant lot, a cluster of children dressed in rags.

Then suddenly she's in a forest. Tall evergreens with straight trunks and beneath them dense undergrowth. No evidence of humans. This must be the Pine

Barrens, she thinks. A half hour passes and another half hour and all she's seen are trees. It's unlike anyplace she's ever been. She checks the mirror and notices a car a long way back. Is it the maroon coupe? When she looks again it's gone. Then, just as she's beginning to get frightened, the town of Hosford comes into view.

There's not much to it—fewer stores and offices than on a single block in Queens. You'd think the powerful Stratemeyer company could find a better place to do business. It's now shortly after noon. She made good time, even with the detour to lose the maroon coupe. But now where is she supposed to go? She'd been counting on Frank to tell her. She'll have to ask someone for help.

She parks and enters a café. It's one of the few establishments on the street that looks open. But inside there's no one sitting at the tables, no one behind the counter, not a single soul. The air smells of old grease and cigarette smoke. The only sound is the ticking of a clock. Just as she's about to turn and go back out the door, a man emerges from the kitchen. He's wearing a dirty apron and holding a spatula in his left hand.

"Can I help you?" he asks.

"I hope so. I'm looking for a woman. Her name is Inez Maddox. She came here from the city to work."

"To Hosford?"

"Yes. She's a detective. A girl detective. As am I."

The man looks skeptical. "Inez, huh? I might know her. There's an Inez who comes in here sometimes."

"Well I need to talk to her. She hasn't been showing up for work. I want to find out why."

"I think she's . . . I think she's keeping time with a guy. Are you her kid?"

"Me? No. She doesn't have any kids. And if she did they wouldn't be as old as me. But are you saying she got married? That would be against the rules."

He shakes his head. "Married? Not even close."

Things are moving along well. She's getting lots of information and nothing is more useful than information. It's how mysteries get solved. She glances at her watch, the white-gold one her father gave her. She might be able to wrap this up and get back in time for supper, maybe put the car in the garage before her father gets home.

"Do you know where I can find her?"

The man frowns. He seems to be deciding how involved he wants to get. Daisy gives him her special smile, the one that says *I'm the most trustworthy teenager you've ever met.*

"Yeah, okay. Here's what you do. Keep on Main until you reach the Esso garage. Then take a right. In about a block the road turns to dirt. You'll pass an oak tree with a tire swing hanging off it. The next house is the one you're looking for.

It's gray with a broken door. Leave your car here if you want. It's an easy walk."

On foot the town looks even more decrepit than it did when viewed from the car. Display windows are empty or, if there are items remaining, they're covered with dust and dead flies. She passes a shoe store that looks open, a hair salon that's closed, and an insurance office that looks as though someone tried to set it on fire. At the Esso station where she's supposed to turn there's a man in overalls working on a car. He hears her footsteps, glances up, and goes back to working on the car.

Once she's made the turn she thinks maybe she should have driven. After ten minutes of walking the road has yet to turn to dirt. But finally it does and she can see an enormous oak up ahead.

The gray house is not very nice. Certainly none in her neighborhood in Queens are in such poor condition. It could use a new roof. Somebody should plant some grass. As Daisy approaches the door she wonders what Inez is doing here and why she stopped showing up for work. As the man at the cafe said, the screen door is half off its hinges. She holds it aside with one hand while with the other she knocks. A few seconds later her co-worker, her replacement, her alter ego, is standing before her.

"Oh, Inez, I'm so glad you're here," Daisy says. "Mr. Stratemeyer sent me to bring you back. Everyone is worried about you. I don't suppose you've figured out who's been stealing horses? I'm anxious to get this case solved."

But something's wrong. "Do I know you?" Inez asks.

Daisy steps back. "I'm Daisy from work. Daisy Frost. Remember, we agreed to switch places. So you've been Daisy Frost for a while." Inez doesn't look well. Her hair has gone back to being limp and brown instead of blonde and bouncy, her eyes have no light in them, and she's wearing a dress that might once have been yellow but is now scarcely any color at all.

Inez shakes her head. "That's not me. You've got the wrong person. My name isn't Inez. Or Daisy. I've never seen you before."

For a moment Daisy finds this unnerving. *What if I'm not who I think I am?* But of course she is. Who else could she be?

"May I use your phone? I need to call home." She wants to tell Hazel she'll be late for supper. More importantly, she knows from experience that asking to use the phone is a good way to gain entry to someone's house.

"We don't have a phone"

"Oh. Well, that's okay. Look, maybe our changing places didn't work out. I'll take you back to the city with me. You can finish writing the book and I'll come out here and look for the horse thieves. How does that sound? Have you seen Cousin Bill lately? He's supposed to help solve this case."

"Listen to me, girly, and listen good. I don't know anything about horses or Cousin Bill. You're starting to piss me off."

"But Inez...." In the dark room behind her she can see a man in a rocking chair. He's wearing a white t-shirt and smoking a cigarette. He hasn't shaved in a while. And then it comes to her. The guy at the café was wrong. Inez *is* married. She's hiding out because she's broken one of the rules. The most important one. But maybe not. Suppose Inez is living with a man and *not* married? The rules say nothing about such an arrangement but surely it's prohibited. And yet, if it's not on the list of rules can it still be a rule? The rules, which seemed logical at first glance, are actually rather confusing. On the table beside the man is a beer bottle. On the dusty hardwood floor, in a spot of sunshine, a white cat is sleeping. The beer is clearly an infraction but what about the cat? She's known good people to own cats. The cat rule is a stupid rule.

While she's having these thoughts, whatever little patience Inez had left has disappeared. "Get the hell off my porch," she says and slams the door.

Daisy begins walking away. Under her breath she says, *Fucking bitch*. Then she stops and looks back. At that moment her detective instincts spring to life. This is all extremely suspicious. There's something shady going on.

She pretends to continue toward town but when she's past the oak tree she circles back and hides behind a dilapidated fence. After creeping through some overgrown shrubbery, she positions herself against the side of the house, beneath an open window. From there she can hear them talking inside:

"Stop saying that. She believed me. I know she did."

"I'm not so sure. Isn't she supposed to be some kind of detective?"

"Not anymore. She gave it up."

"But her old man has money?"

"Yes."

"How much?"

"I told you he's a lawyer. He's loaded."

"And you're sure we can find their house in Queens?"

Daisy has heard enough. This has all been a setup. She needs to get back to the car.

She pushes through the shrubbery again and runs down the dirt road toward Main Street. It's getting late, the sun turning red as it falls behind the trees. When she reaches the Esso station, the man in overalls is locking up for the night. This time he doesn't notice as she passes. The shoe store has closed as well and the lights in the café are off.

As she approaches the car something doesn't look right. It seems to have gotten lower to the ground. Now she can see the problem: the front tire on the driver's side is flat. Slashed, probably with a knife. The same thing has been done to the rear tire. She continues around to the opposite side. The other two are flat as well.

In the time she's been inspecting the tires, darkness has continued to fall.

She looks from one end of the street to the other. Not a single person in sight. Maybe she can find Cousin Bill. If he actually exists. How's she going to get home? Or if not, where can she spend the night? She's never had to do this before. Her father won't come looking for her because he doesn't know where she went. A stray dog crosses the street. Where's the good person who owns it? Her mind is swirling, a mixture of confusion and fear, and her eyes are filling with tears. Mr. Stratemeyer could do something about this if he wanted to. Her world was invented by Mr. Stratemeyer. He can alter it in any way he chooses. Why has he placed her in danger? Why is she all alone?

She takes a breath and tells herself to focus. This case is going to be challenging but she's certain she can crack it. Daisy Frost can crack it. Because that's who she is and what she does. Up the street a car appears. Although she's half-blinded by the headlights she thinks it must be the maroon coupe. Between now and when it reaches her, she'll come up with a plan. She always does best under pressure. Now the car is fully visible. She'd hide but it's too late. The maroon coupe is on its way.

CORAZONES DE PAPEL

Luis Lopez-Maldonado

Part I: Land Before Democracy
We wereare ancient dreamers, our backs heavy with discrimination our walls infested with crucifixes our brown little dreamers rejecting the term dreamers calling out the white people on their racism fascism leftism fake journalism, because activism is cool Instagram worthy and high school teachers with their high school books continue teaching Christopher Columbus discovered America white teachers reaffirming that their democracy is fair and correct and powerful and honest and real,

Part II: ~~Republicans~~ Guns Kill People
In less than a minute

at the first slap across face,
kick to ribs, yank of hair,
blue bruise to brown skin:

ten thousand *poemas*
would have already been lived

I praise life. Because I'm still here.
Still gay. Still brown.
Still free:

USA: let's go to school:
shot, to the mall: shot,
pray at church: shot,

twerk at a gay club: shot,
get some frozen pizzas
at Wal-Mart: shot,
how 'bout music concert:
shot, a morning yoga class:

shot,

COLLECTING MEDICINE

Kurt Schweigman

As a young man
back in '95 cradled
into burgundy cracked vinyl
one hand steering wheel driving
my '75 Rez Cadillac El Dorado
on the summer high plains
gathering afternoon sun blue sky
left forearm relaxing
on the open driver's door window sill
long flowing hair in the dust heat wind
imitation Ray Ban shades on
beat-up baseball hat low to the brow
cig dangling from my thin Sioux lips
    like a cool guy
tooling around my hometown
for no particular reason
sometimes I just loved taking
my dinosaur war pony metal beast out
    on a sunny summer day

Suddenly this time and moment
thinking of my Lakota ancestors
    in no particular way
turning a city corner
from a traffic busy street
a small rock jumped through
my open moon roof
into the pocket of my shirt

As an old man now
the stone was lost long ago
    but not its torque meaning
Rez Caddy power plant grinded away
until piston rods knocking
just before its own death
a 500 cubic inch V8 engine block
pavement crushing machine

MAINLANDERS

K-Ming Chang

When the mainlanders moved into the back unit, my mother told me not to talk to them, eat with them, or lend them money. Don't open your mouth around flies, she said. She duct-taped the lids of our plastic bins before trash day in case they shoved their dirty diapers to the bottom of our bins or fished out our recyclables. That's what mainlanders are like, my mother said, saddling us all with their shit. These mainlanders were the Zhangs, the same last name as me, though mine was spelled differently and had no man attached to it. My mother said that my name was quilted together the right way, and that their name was a product of dressing up letters as soldiers and lining them up with guns to their backs, coercing them into a row. The Zhangs were made up of one baba, one mama, one jiejie, one meimei, one nainai, one yeye, and one guma—a shame, my mother said, that mainlanders all live on top of each other like that. You know how it is, people are cheap in China, that's the one thing that doesn't cost any money there, people! And look, all girls! my mother said, when she saw them slip one at a time out of the white van. You know mainlanders are barbarians who used to drown their baby girls, she said, I saw it on TV, a documentary about drowning girls in piss pots, and that was in the '80s! Because a piss pot is the easiest water within reach. Those girls don't even get the dignity of drowning in a pond or a river or even a goddamn sink! My mother was always complaining about our plumbing, which she said was already clogged up by the Zhangs, who must be flushing something alive down the toilet, though the only time I'd ever seen the Zhangs use water is when they filled up a daisy-patterned kiddie pool in their backyard with water and took turns jumping in together, even the nainai and guma who had bad knees, the girls laughing so loud all the crows fled from the trees and canceled out the sky and I could stand forever in their dark, watching. My mother told me she heard it on the news channel, that story about a woman on the mainland who killed an old man, a man who was married and had a family and was paying to touch her—though remember, she was the one who approached him because she was in debt from so much shopping, a symptom of mainlander materialism, my mother said—and minced his corpse into pork, bought a pressure-cooker, and stewed his flesh, then flushed all his bits down the toilet. When the apartment downstairs complained of clogging, the plumber opened up the pipes and discovered over 10,000 bits of flesh! Can you believe! my mother said. For a week she watched the story on TV, her eyes sipping all light from the screen, and in the mornings, I tip-toed out of the house and drank water out of the hose outside so she wouldn't wake from the sofa. After last week, when our toilet burbled like a phlegmy throat and the water in our tap was so thick it shrugged in the sink, solidifying pink, my mother said she was afraid to call the landlord, who would call the plumber, who might discover something sick in our pipes. I didn't tell her it was me who flushed three fists of toilet paper down the toilet after Mandy Hsia told me about how she induced her period by shoving a mechanical Oxi-gel pencil between her legs and twisting it to turn the blood on like a tap. I tried, but just with a Bic pen, which only caused a slow trickling like our faucet that's always been bad, and because I didn't want my mother to see the tissues I polka-dotted—I asked her once how to get my period, and she said I shouldn't ask about things so dirty, then turned on the TV—I flushed the paper all at once. Mandy Hsia has a mainland mother that I met once after softball practice—she brought everyone egg-and-pork-floss sandwiches, which I didn't know mainlanders ate too—and later, when my mother picked me up, I told her that Mandy's mother said ni men chi wan le ma? with her tongue curled all the way in like a snail in its shell. My mother said, Ah, a mainland wife, you know that's all Taiwanese men go for these days, those whores, you know they sell themselves? Taiwanese women, we're too independent for them, they all run to the nearest spread legs. So I asked my mother, is that why baba isn't here, and maybe if I sat with my legs spread, baba would come back? My mother reached back to slap my leg in the passenger seat, the only time she ever touched me, and said I didn't know shit, and when we got home, we ate side-by-side on the sofa with the TV on, our pipes scratching open their throats in the background. My mother always watched one channel with a man who stood in front of a blue screen and liked to shout a lot and point at things, a little like baba before he left, and he said, Scandal! The Pot Has Boiled Over! Last week a mainland tourist was caught crouching with her daughter in the middle of a mall, and her daughter was peeing into a diaper she held open, just like that, peeing in front of the whole public! And now here is the footage of the incident, taken by a local university student, and see how the mother knocks the man's phone out of his hands and even refuses to pay for it, now watch, the girl opening her legs in front of the whole world like she's got no family name!

My mother turned the volume up, a column of sound between us, and I wondered if the Zhangs on the other side of the wall could hear us, the way I could hear their bowls clattering on the dinner table or the ache of a mattress spring beneath their bodies, and the man on screen was jutting his finger between the girl's legs, her Tweety Bird skirt foaming up around her, his finger pinning her there forever, but it wasn't the girl I was looking at, it was the mother crouched in front of her, the way she cradled the open diaper in her palms, offering it up like an island, shifting it a little to the right to catch the glimmering necklace of piss, her seismic hands, the way she was whispering something to her daughter, too quiet for me to hear even when I leaned in, the way she bent so close their foreheads were almost touching, their widow's peaks matching, her shadow a tent around them both, as if to say I am the only one you will ever need to see, for as long as you need, I will hold all your heat, I will keep the world at your feet.

ABUELITA'S PRAYERS

Jose Hernandez Diaz

After my Abuelita prayed for me, I was suddenly cured of all susto. I no longer feared small talk at the grocery store. I no longer feared standing in front of an audience and reciting depressing poetry. After my Abuelita made the sign of the cross on my forehead, I let go of all irrational fear. I applied for jobs I was barely qualified for. I had the confidence of a mediocre white man. I could win them over in the interview, I thought. My Abuelita, the darkest one in the family, the one I resemble the most, from Michoacán. She cured me. I am no longer afraid. Susto, no longer part of my vocabulary. I march along, beneath the sun, ready to conquer: Adelante, siempre Adelante.

ARRANGED MARRIAGE

Susan Calvillo

Gorillas sense the strain
of arranged marriage as well
as any bride, sister, or child
who enters into such a union
without giving their consent.
When presented with her suitor
—a 400-pound silverback—
the leading lady of this story
did not skip off
to a whitewashed chapel,
tremble down a petal-strewn aisle,
or stutter at any altar.
Still, despite the lack of vows
he was released into her meadow.
The ones who loved her most
tried to explain to her:
We're doing this for you.
We only want to see you happy.
But when he touched her
it was not joy she felt
but the sense of duty
the legacy she was to gift
this chosen mate, this foundation,
the world.
From the moment she saw him
it was clear he was willing

to play his part.
Could he help that it was
in his nature? It was
what they shipped him here to do.
But this was *her* sanctuary.
This was her *body*.
She ran the show.
The shriek that followed
was a different kind of consent:
the plea for death before rape.
She sank her teeth into him
accepting the consequences.
She tried to tear him to shreds.
They've been living
in separate trailers ever since.

POETRY IS THE ONLY REAL MOTHER

after Diane Seuss

Susan Michele Coronel

archangel, bitch, disaster mountain, manna, bowl of mushroom barley soup
  at the Blue Bay Diner, my grandma's potato kugel, how I was content,
pearls of grain paired with firm, shiny mushrooms in broth flecked

with flank meat, potato pie like poetry, the only gold, or was it, my belly button
  pining for its lost umbilical cord as my fingers waggled, my ring finger
floating solo on a trip around my bedroom, fingering myself in the dark,

finger foods on a tray—Ritz crackers layered with Cheese Whiz.
  How could it be that I was a whiz at what is holy? I rode my bike
down the hill without feet, handlebars directing me home to the bottomless hole.

I talked to God and told Him I didn't believe, stared at the T.V. and thought,
  This is more real than my life and this is where I want to be. I wanted
to be loved like Ma and Pa loved Laura on *Little House on the Prairie*

or shack up with Chrissy, Jack, and Janet from *Three's Company*, floating
  down the Long Beach boardwalk like a silly-billy angel melting
in the California sun. Before I talked to God, I was in love with my grandma's touch

and my mother's clutch—at least we were together, though what did we have
  in common? Nothing much. I blew dandelion seeds through the forest,
demanding that lion's tooth be reclassified as flower. *Not weed,*

I told the blackberry king behind the parking garage. Seeds disappeared
  into the sky like tiny, furred balloons. My stuffed animals talked to me,
fur matted like the terry cloth towel my mother wrapped my hair in after a bath,

my plaits sopping dark drips until she blow-dried me, freed me from the burden
    of water so all my skin could be smooth—underarms, ears, forehead, vulva.
I made myself come along the side of the tub. I came on the corner

of the floral bedspread watching *Mister Rogers' Neighborhood* as my mother
    popped frozen dinners in the oven, turkey thighs with carrots, peas
and whipped potatoes with a side of crusty custard. Did I know that a simile

was coming on, did I feel it slip out from between my legs and squeal?
    Does language replace lack, does it pay you back if you give it
every ounce of feeling that you buried and now want back?

CADAVER PINIONS

A.P. Thayer

We are not afraid, though we look it.

It is not fear that makes our heads bob and causes our beaks to twitch. Our eyes do not dilate out of terror.

We are merely alert.

This is how we survive.

When we don't crane our necks and react to every sound, we die.

In ones and twos and threes, we die.

Metal strikes concrete and we flutter away.

But not all of us.

Once again, it is a pink. An older one; we can tell by the smell. He smashes us with the flat of a shovel. Two of us die, though the second takes far longer than the first to stop breathing.

We crowd around, cooing and swarming while he uses the bloodied shovel to dump the water out of our hole, the puddle we bathe in during this heat, until he has destroyed that, too.

We swirl and dive and lament as he gets back into his car, an electric blue shit-box with beads dangling from the rearview mirror.

We settle. Some of us dip our beaks and our toes into the rapidly evaporating water in the dirt. Others peck at the ground around our dead. The car pulls away. He's gone and our work can begin.

Three pinks bicycle through us, kicking. We whirl and flap and spin and dance away, hurried, but not panicked. We do not know fear. We do not fear them.

One of their boots catches us and we see stars, spinning galaxies, entire cosmos beyond our reach. It's a brief journey before we return. Another one of us has fallen, never returning to this reality where the one star shines bright during the day and we have only a dried up puddle to live in.

This time the pinks stick around. They poke at our dead. They laugh. We walk in wide swaths around our puddle, close enough to see what they're doing to the one they took, not close enough to add to the number of deceased. Watching. Waiting.

They get bored and leave, finally.

Under the cover of feathers and swirling bodies, we do our work.

WE ARE FEWER NOW. Every day more of us die.

But every day, we do the work, and though we lose numbers, we do not lose weight.

We are getting slower, too. The former parts of us we bind to ourselves, to reinforce our wings and talons and beaks and bellies, weigh heavy on us. Heavier than they did in life. We cannot flap our wings, we cannot take flight.

But we work on. We are almost finished.

WATER HAS COME to fill our puddle again. We splash and the bones and feathers of our dead weigh some of us down so they too get added back to us, but we are refreshed. The weight of carrying ourselves in this heat is oppressive and the water is cool. We are three. Then two. Then one. We are the weight of all of our dead and our one living, a monstrous amalgamation.

Metal strikes concrete again. A blue shit-box idles by the side of the road. A wrinkled female pink hunches over the steering wheel while her husband pink drags the same shovel toward us.

We do not whirl. We do not duck our heads.

We attack.

BLOOD PEACH

Gloria Frimpong

Illustrator painting
6” × 8”

RUNNING LOW

Shelbey Leco

acrylic on paper
7" × 10"

DECUSSATE

Dorsía Smith Silva

I'm not saying violence isn't wrong, but I understand it.

Mrs. Hayes is quick to remind us:
We should never put our hands on anyone.
Violence is never the answer.
Then she loads the projector.
The film crackles on the screen.
Of muskets and cannons—
instruments from a war where
the thirteen colonies gained their freedom
by killing men in red—
red like bright breasts of birds
red like big-boned leaves on trees.

Why couldn't they ask King George
for their independence?
Carol wants to know.
Didn't they ask nicely?

The film sputterturns to the Civil War
and bombards us with red over blue
and gray garments. Men getting pummeled
and slaves hoping for a quiltwork of freedom.
Slaves that never had a prelude of asking nicely.
Slaves that swept the dust inbreath,
while masters kneed them dreamless.

Mrs. Hayes has her hands on her hips.
Like my own mother.
When the guidance counselor told her
that I would never get accepted by an Ivy League college.
Her eyes stripping Mr. Connor to a bare letter.
His hands on my mother's shoulders
and the firm brushing away of fat fingers.

The woman's patience chafed her legs, but not her voice.
After two hours of waiting for the doctor,
she screamed and pounded her fists at the counter.
The doctor will see you now, the receptionist's eyes
widened into black moons.
Then a buzz to let her through.
The rest of us clutching our shell-shocked papers.

The group of men circled the heart-shaped train rider,
until she spit-shined a knife and caught a rib.
The men dodged like rodeo clowns.

I think of my mother.
The neighbors when they were told
their children threw stones and dirt into our pool.
My mother's tongue slicing them in a stroke ending.
Her tongue taking the place of fists.
Tell us when to send the cleanup crew, they say.

I understand violence.
It starts as the introduction to many wounds.
You could press down hard enough, if one bleeds:
Aiyana
Atatiana
Breonna
Fred
Malcolm
Martin
Medgar
Sandra
Trayvon
Yvette

They killed our best people.

Until the mouths no longer hold stones,
when the hands are pure,
red will be a color
as good
with good
across good.

KHOUF

for amir, hassib, and massood

Antony Fangary

never forget your mother woke you that morning / you ran to the tv / she said *explosions* / a
tower collapsing into itself / a structure of sand / aware where you stood / how flags can flash
like hammers / fabric and colors can beg / never forget learning you were *arab* / the first time
letters collapsed onto you like soil / never forget hating yourself / your food / music / name
/ what burnt / knuckle / hair smelt like / your mother dyed her hair blonde / plucked your eye
brows into slivers / never forget the wet wrinkle of her scream when the second tower fell / that
it meant something was to come / your parents changed their names / airplanes / random security

checks / being accused of trying to start a caliphate / learning the word *caliphate* / the photo of pope shenouda / the trigger pull that followed / never forget learning about afghanistan / iraq / saudi arabia / iran / palistine / how you / your persian friend / your afghan friend started a tagging crew called *arabs with attitude* / though none of you were arab / white kids wanted to join / you told them they had to get jumped/in / how easily abdomens give in to driving knees / how pink white flesh can flush / when they first said *never forget* and how bad you wished they would / when your friend/s dad said *they need to just nuke all the fuckin arabs* / how stiff his jaw looked / the terror in your father/s eyes when he saw you wearing a shirt that said *diamond* in arabic / how he calls you every time there is a mass/shooter / how he begs you to shave your face / how 14 people were killed near your house in san bernardino / he begs you to shave your face / never forget when your father told you that we deserve this / we changed the way the world travels / no other people have done this before / we have nothing to be proud of

ONLY THE DEAD GO TO HEAVEN

Matthew Moniz

Sign every correspondence
with an albatross quill,
still red-flecked from its harvest.
Denouement is stasis;
living things rip, tear,
repeat, repair, accumulate.
Squeeze a stone until generosity
drips out, a trick of the inner light—
cups and balls, loaves and fishes.
Consume. Poop. Do it again.

It's okay that stars burn out,
because when they do, they explode.
It's okay that when dawn comes,
the nearest star swallows all others.
Order is a symptom of chaos
and pain is a signal of life—
bones stretch, brains
strain, and skin flexes when used.
It's okay that some explosions are small.
Leave things leavened. The dough needs violence
to rise.
Move. Move again. Wiggle
like a fat tadpole ready for legs.
Float fetally against a mattress
and fall asleep to write with dream logic.
Climb into the topiary rictus,
snap a branch, and let it lie.
Rearrange the pieces.
Breathing rips the air apart
and shoots chunks of selves
back out. Thermodynamics
don't care one bit about
sitting still. Every little friction
is an undoing. Pare parables,
paradise, pareidolia.

Roil. Boil. Explode.
Perfection is an end—
it never means well.
Ten minutes till pens down,
          till the quill goes horizontal.
So be as saintly as you like—
                              but whatever it is, it does
                                        not have to be finished—

ANOTHER PLACE

Rachel Deutsch

THE WEEK I WENT ACROSS town to stay with my grandparents, I had a secret. The secret was buried under my clothes, deep in my belly. Small as a raspberry, but growing every day, moving up the fruit food chain in size. I didn't want anyone to know, and my mom would be suspicious if I was puking all the time, so my plan was to hide out at my grandparents for a couple days until I could get the abortion. I was sixteen.

My grandpa called himself James, but his real name was Velvel, which means wolf in Yiddish. He used the Anglo name like a shield. Like it could possibly conceal his origins. I imagined him walking the streets of Montreal with a "James" name tag clipped to his Rabbinical beard and thinking to himself: "That'll trick 'em." My grandma's name was Faiga, which means little bird, even though she was big and solid. When I asked her if she'd ever change her name like him, she flapped her arms like wings and laughed like a car starting up in the winter.

My grandparents cooked with so much onion that my eyes watered as soon as I stepped into their apartment. It was as if they were working hard to ward off evil spirits. I went to sit in the kitchen. I was dizzy from the heat on the street, but inside it was no better. Grandma Faiga came to kiss the top of my head, her giant breasts brushing into my face, and Grandpa James winked at me from across the table. The few hairs on the top of his head were blowing in the wind, like they were in a different place, in different weather. Like usual, there was soup boiling on the stove. I knew that if I reached for the lid, my grandma would whack my hand. It was always a secret what was in the pot. The wallpaper next to the stove was stained with something from a hundred years ago. It had slowly faded to a curious gold color, looking classier over time.

The rattle of the stockpot on the stove was doing something to my stomach.

I excused myself to go throw up in the toilet. The tiles on the bathroom floor were cool against my knees. I wiped down the toilet seat and opened the window so the smell would go out. When I came back to the kitchen, my grandma stared at me for a moment and scrunched up her nose. Then she turned back to cooking. I sat in a chair across from Grandpa James. His shirt was popping open and I could see his gaping, hairy belly button. It was hard not to look.

He loved playing a game in which he rapped his knuckles on the table and made me slap his wrists. I didn't understand the rules so he always won, and he celebrated by wagging a finger in my face and shouting, "Ha!"

Grandma Faiga wore little heels at home that scratched up the floors. Instead of making her legs look longer, they somehow accentuated her thick ankles. When she saw me looking, she slipped them off to do a shuffle dance. Her brown stockings hung a little from her toes, and she tucked her dress up under her heavy breasts and put her fists on her hips. It was some kind of peasant dance. Grandpa James went to the other room to turn the record player up and then returned to hit the table, speeding up and slowing down in time with her footwork and the music. From what I could tell, the singer was repeating, "Yadada ba ba ba ba ba," very fast.

When the dance was finished, my grandpa laughed exuberantly and thumped her bum as if she were a horse who had just won a competition. They left the record blaring. With that music as their daily soundtrack, no wonder they were how they were. Like they were always changing tempo.

I put my head in my hands because I was feeling sick again.

At night, I slept on their couch. They had a metal fan in the window that was meant to pull the outside night air in, but it wasn't making it any cooler. I could hear both of them snoring in the other room. My grandpa's was a whistle and my grandma's, a grating in her throat. They both slept in sleeveless nightshirts and boxy shorts with their feet hanging off the end of their bed. Because all their furniture was small, they always seemed giant until they stepped outside. In the night, I woke up to my grandma's dry hand on my forehead. "You have bad dreams," she whispered and blew on my face.

The morning of the appointment, I dressed in the bathroom and put on a long skirt and my "hide and squeak" shirt with a picture of a mouse hiding from another mouse. I thought shorts wouldn't be formal enough for the situation, but I was already starting to sweat. I took a long time washing my face with cold water in their tiny sink and then I drew a thin line of makeup along my upper eyelids.

When I finally came out, my grandma was wearing a flowery green dress and her scarf. She had her outside shoes on. They were the kind some old people wore that looked like velcro toddler shoes.

"I'm coming with you," she said. I froze.

"Grandma, I have to be somewhere. An appointment."

She opened the door and went to stand in the hallway. I thought I could get rid of her on the way, drop her off at some fruit market and run off down the street. But I didn't. She came with me, rocking into me on the metro and clutching my arm on the escalators for balance.

When we got to the clinic I asked her to wait in the park across the street. I thought she would say no and insist on coming in with me, but she crossed the street slowly and went to sit on a bench near the fountain. She looked like a Russian nesting doll from far away, her dress over her knees and her little scarf knotted tightly under her neck. She sat up very straight.

My baby was a tiny black hole in the whirling white of the ultrasound. I watched it disappear from the screen. A thing that was there and then wasn't. I cried for it and for me and for everything in this life that was too small and/or far too big. I cried for all the things that I couldn't have and for all the things I wouldn't be. I cried until my hair was wet around my face like a crown and then I stopped. All the holes in the ceiling panels looked like stars in a galaxy, and the thing that I lost and the things I would later have were just dots above me.

Afterwards, I slumped in the chair in the recovery room until I could stand up properly enough so they'd let me leave. I had to promise the nurse that someone was waiting for me to take me home. She narrowed her eyes at me like she didn't believe me. Then she softly touched my arm and said, "Take care dear."

When I got outside, Grandma Faiga was sitting on the steps of the building. A lone protester with a sign that read, "Jesus is watching," was staring her down from the other side of the street. Grandma waved at them with the back of her hand, as if she was chasing a fly from her food.

I was wobbly, and she grabbed onto my arm, holding me up this time around. We crossed back to the park and sat down on the same bench. She pulled a container from her bag. It was soup with lots of green stuff in it and, of course, onions.

"It will help with the bleeding." She smiled softly and handed me a spoon. "These things were not so safe in the old days. A girl in my village...." Her voice trailed off and we stared at each other until I looked down.

I ate a bit, but was so groggy from the morphine that my eyes kept closing. She took my cheeks in her rough hands and then put her arm around me and pulled me to her shoulder. We watched the spray from the fountain shoot into air and then fall into the pool before it was sucked through the drain to start the cycle again. My grandma smelled of another place, far across the ocean, and was so soft that resting on her was like floating on water.

PROMISED LAND

Nicole Lachat

In this country I'm wind-slapped

Red stain that will not dry

Elbow-deep in sand and earth

Begging stones to water[1]

Mamá

I hear you calling me

Sleep disposes of me like a cannon

Sweat and silence land me

I gasp for air

I'm glad you're not here

Here is full of scorpions

Here the desert crossing is 500 years

And counting

[1]Exodus 17:6

HELP

after Noor Hindi

Krystle May Statler

I'm not a curl anymore—
I've straightened too many strands.
All they do is break away.
Unremarkable news, I'm unremarkable
in my recent hair loss.
I have dates on my calendar
just for crying. I do this
between my 6–3. *Help. Help.*
I'm angrier than I seem.
I'm a bullet in a temple.
Please close the damn window.
Please tell my mother
I'm tired of forgiving.
My desire to fix this hole is rotten.
Her desire to deny our loss
with guilt's repetition,
is an act of the grieving mother.
At the mortuary, a stranger hugged me like a mother.
Please, no, I hugged her back. I don't hope
anymore. I do the job as daughter
(angry, loving) from afar. I cradle
the hole. I fight
my relapse into a reminder
then kiss a unicorn urn.
My father wears a cross
on his neck.

A lacerated family mess.
Brother, please, show a sign.
My memories are losing blood.

THE WARS IN MY MOTHER

Nathan Truong

My mother is a good mother when she wants to be. In front of the pastor, she'll prop me up, polish me, lick a finger to slick back my hair and some of my failures so that I look like my imagined self. The pastor looks at me and thinks he sees me, blesses me. But I take those blessings and drown them in the holy water on the way out. She tells me not to stay out past nine. She flinches every time she hears a loud bang. It's just the kids, I say. A skateboard smashed on the sidewalk. She doesn't sleep. She has never slept. Not since the church pulled her body out of the Pacific because her sea legs were hungry for land. When a nun dried her eight-year-old body on a rock, she thought America was that single rock. She didn't know the world could be so big. Time on the water diminishes days into a strong enough singular so that there is no before or after. Simply still on that rock, she let time account for itself in her body.

1 a.m. all the Heinekens burping out of me in every misstep but his kisses still stink on my upper lip with maraschino cherry puke climbing through the window splinters caught in the blue of my jeans and there is my mother in the dark in the kitchen whispering a name that is not my own Bùi "Bùi, don't go, keep hiding, here in the dirt," at the corner of the living room, I listen, hear crying, see no tears, she's sleepwalking but she is so still she is a wall, thick plaster barrier, buoyed by blessings, the ones I thought I killed, bring me close to her and I ask if she's okay, but she cannot hear me past her blank stare, and slowly, like a midnight wave, she laps and laps back to bed and I am dark in the kitchen, unheard and far from that kiss.

White rice noodles pull apart so that they don't stick. Her hands move faster than she thinks. In my split mother tongue, I ask, "Who is Bùi?" She says she knows no one by that name. What I do know is that with a different intonation, bùi could mean dust. "You said her name in your dream last night." I dreamed?

"You dreamed. You told her to hide." She doesn't exist, my mother says. She plops the noodles into bowls and tops them all with a thick bone broth. We sit to eat and the TV is on blast, a newswoman speaking softly about a murder. I string noodles into my mouth and stop. There is a third bowl when it's only my mother and I. She pays no attention, listening to the woman. I leave to the bathroom to look at myself in the mirror, touching my lips with the sides of my fingers so that I'm given attention, so that the reflection in the mirror is a portrait. My arms stretch out with the weight of the care I've always wanted from my mother and hold myself, hold dust, whoever she is. But care turns into concern and my hands tremble with some kind of future arthritis, brittle, bùi. I come back to my mother and the third bowl is emptied. She has bills in her hands and furrows in her brows. She left burning sugarcane fields for this. My English and my time are limited, she says. "Did you finish two bowls?" Only one. She looks at me, finally. It was for the past. The past is hungry too.

WE BURY OUR DEAD SO WHITE PEOPLE HAVE THINGS TO DISCOVER

Rémy Ngamije

Listen,
the ancestors say:

> Carve the coffins
> from living wood and
> adorn them with your tears.
>
> Or hue them from rock
> and the bones of the earth,
> better suited for carrying
> a thousand-year grief.

Listen,
the ancestors declare:

> Sing the songs of mourning,
> noon and night and back around
> again when dawn and dusk are merely
> the difference between sobbing and shrieking.
>
> Weep, from the nadir of death
> to the zenith of your agony,
> and let it be known: you have lost.

Listen,
the ancestors command:

Honour the rituals: remove the brains,
the tongue, the soft bits; encase the dead vessel
in linen; line its bed with hunting bows,
trinkets, silver, and gold.

Listen,
the ancestors whisper:

If you are smart, set it all alight—
Reduce everything you love to smoke and
let it glide through the air and
make each breeze a tombstone.

Listen,
the ancestors laugh:

We bury our dead so that white people have
things to discover.

Hell is lying with your shrivelled dick and
crooked bones in a glass coffin in London.

WE EXCHANGED FLOWERS

Claire Lawrence

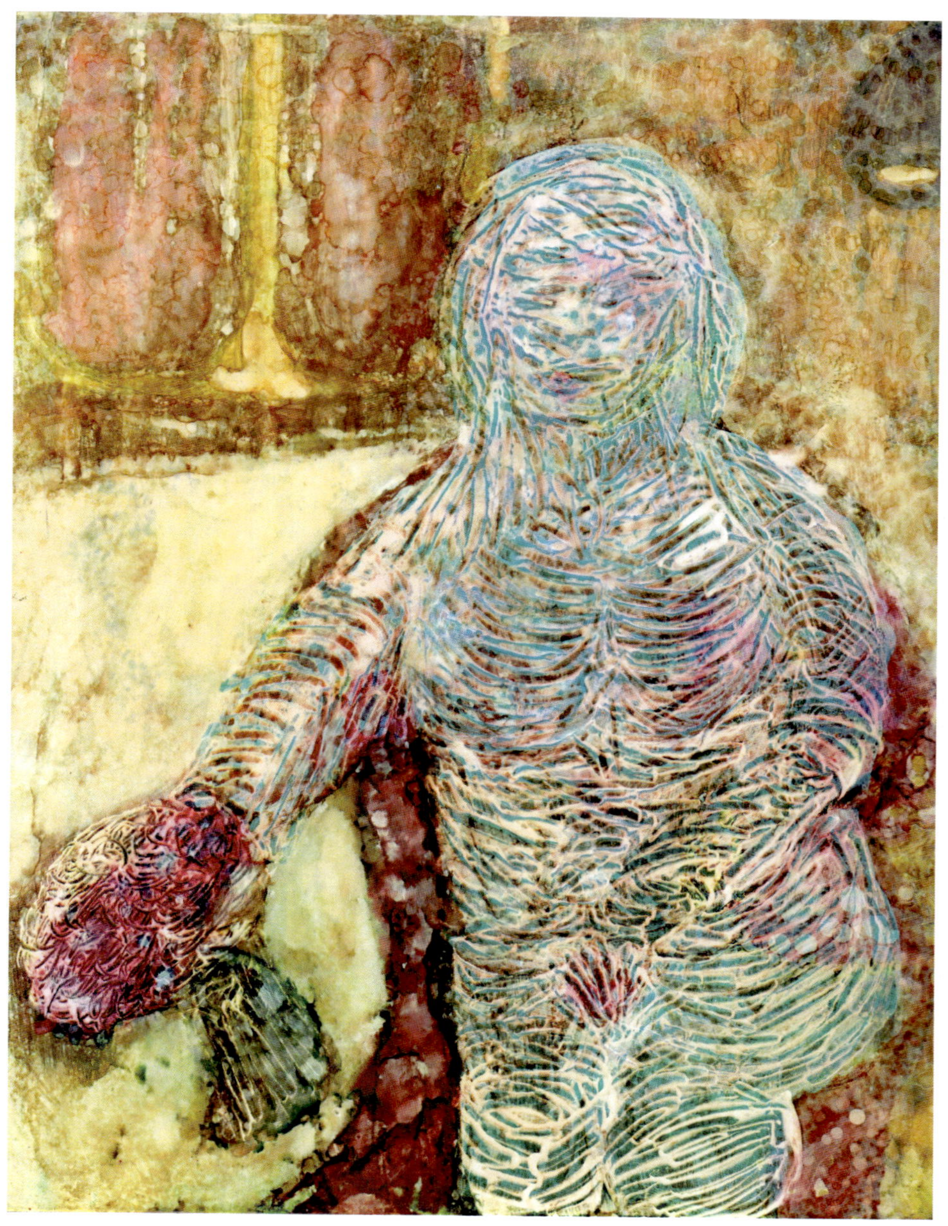

acrylic and alcohol ink on Yupo paper
8.5" × 11"

BEAUTIFUL PRISONERS

Lena Zycinsky

acrylic and collage on canvas
40" × 60"

JOHN TRAVOLTA VS FARRAH FAWCETT

Hiram Perez

[CONTENT WARNING: *contains offensive language*]

My sister Miracle and her best friend Blanca spend most of their time worshipping John Travolta and reading Barbara Cartland novels. Their love for Travolta confuses me. The girls on Yolanda Hernández's guagua go crazy for him too. The other day, my friend Hector's twin sister Helen got on the bus with a John Travolta duo-tang—the kind with twin pockets but no fasteners. Davia Novoa and Patty Gonzalez shrieked.

"Niñas," Yolanda snapped, shushing them.

She arched her orange eyebrow and looked into the rearview mirror. All of us know Yolanda sees everything in that mirror. The way she says "niñas" means *shut up* but also *this is not how young ladies behaved in Cuba*. When she says "niñas" like that, I picture girls in frilly dresses, not the tight Sassoon jeans that Davia and Patty wear all the time. Yolanda's scolding quieted the whole bus. Helen and Hector, who are always quiet anyway, stood in the aisle because there weren't enough seats. I looked at the folder Helen held against her chest trying to figure out the big deal. Travolta looked back at me with puppy dog eyes. He wore a leather vest on top of a white dress shirt unbuttoned to show off the chest hair growing two inches under the tan line on his neck. I stared at his chest hair and then turned to check for Yolanda's eye in the rearview mirror. Travolta's long, feathered hair made his face look even longer.

I still can't understand why girls go so crazy for him. Mami says men shouldn't have long hair. Only hippies and maricónes have long hair. She has strong opinions about how men should look. I agree with her about men with long hair except for Randolph Mantooth, who plays fireman John Gage on *Emergency!* I like how thick and black his hair looks. I like how the corners of his mouth curve down in the same direction as the outside corners of his eyes.

Miracle is turning thirteen and lords those extra five years over me. Half the questions I ask, she says, "You're too young to know." She can tell how crazy that makes me. I'm angry because I want to be included. Especially since she went to West Miami Junior High last year and left me behind at Coral Terrace. "With the babies," she says. Sharing a bed with her little brother only makes Miracle resent me more. I am desperate to learn what she and Blanca whisper about. Sometimes they fall on the bed laughing after sharing a secret. I watch from the doorway hypnotized by their almost-teenage girl ways. They crack each other up with their fake English accents pretending to be Fleur and Norman from Barbara Cartland's *Escape from Passion*. But it does not take long for them to return to their favorite topic: men. Especially Erik Estrada, John Travolta, and Snapper from *The Young and the Restless*. When our half-sister Zoraida takes us to see *Smokey and the Bandit*, we watch a trailer for *The Goodbye Girl*, and Miracle whispers, "We have to see that." But she keeps quiet for the next preview. A pair of shiny red shoes walks toward us, keeping the beat to the Bee Gees' "Stayin' Alive." The camera travels up a pair of black pants and then a black jacket over a red shirt. It's Travolta. His hair is shorter. Miracle stops blinking. I know because after the first few seconds, I watch her instead of the screen. I want to take in her excitement. I want to be a part of it. I want to see what she sees with those not-blinking, almost-teenage girl eyes. After *Smokey and the Bandit*, Miracle and I take turns writing down the words to the Bee Gees' "How Deep Is Your Love" whenever it plays on Y-100, which is all the time basically. I decide to buy Miracle a John Travolta poster for her birthday, using the money I made helping Papi at the boat factory all summer. Maybe Blanca and Miracle will start sharing their secrets with me, I think. Maybe I won't be "too young to know" anymore.

Papi complains when I ask him to take me shopping for Miracle's poster, even though I let him sleep late. It's rare for him to have a day off, even on a Sunday. Westchester queda cerquita, I plead. We are less than ten minutes away. There are bigger, fancier malls in Miami, but I prefer Westchester. Miracle's favorite, Dadeland, feels too big and crowded and expensive. There's even a store at Dadeland that only sells Lladró porcelains. Mami always makes us stop and stare through the window at the clowns and ballerinas with their long necks while she tells us in a sad voice how much she dreams of one day owning a Lladró. Then she sucks her teeth and walks away. Each time I stay at the window a few extra seconds, picking out the pieces I will buy for Mami when I'm rich. At Westchester Mall you can walk into any store without feeling poor. There is a Pantry Pride on one end and Kmart on the other. I like how if you enter through the Kmart side you can smell the pet store right away. It's always dark inside Westchester except for the bright light from the fake Orange Julius where you can get Cuban empanadas. We call the Orange Julius drink a morir soñando, which means to die dreaming. It's one of Papi's favorites. Sometimes he makes his own at home, dumping Tang, vanilla ice cream, milk, and ice cubes into the blender. The promise of a to-die-dreaming finally coaxes him to drive us to the mall.

I feel my father's thick hand on my shoulder as we enter through the glass doors nearest to the fake Orange Julius. Papi works as a boat carpenter. He is a short, square man with hands and forearms too thick for his build. His skin is the color of old pennies. I am paler than both Papi and Cuca, my mother of Filipino blood, born in Cienfuegos, which means one hundred fires. She was pregnant with me when they left Cienfuegos for Miami, but I don't think I inherited any of the fire. My color makes me ashamed. It is too soft, just like everything about me.

Our destination is the store across from the Orange Julius, the one that reminds me of the drawing of a bazaar from a book I checked out of the library called *Caravan*. They sell the Billboard Chart's top ten singles at ninety-nine cents and posters for five dollars. After the pet shop, it's my favorite store at Westchester. The bazaar also sells giant vases decorated with ostrich feathers dyed the same orange and aqua as the Miami Dolphins colors, ancient keys that look like they were found in a shipwreck, and playing-card sized framed copies of the *Mona Lisa* and a painting called *The Blue Boy*. Papi gently squeezes my shoulder as we walk inside. The clerk, an older Cuban man, asks how he can help us and I point to the poster, the famous one with Travolta in white pointing to the disco gods.

My father laughs as he protests, "That's not the one you want." He points instead to the poster of Farrah Fawcett in a red one-piece bathing suit, smiling at us with her white teeth. "Don't you want that one?"

Confused, I explain, "But it's for Miri."

"So what?" he protests again. "That's the poster you should buy." From the direction his eyes stare, I can tell he is not so much talking to me as making his case for the clerk.

"But it's her birthday. This is a birthday present for Miri."

"¿Y qué? Debes comprar ese," he repeats. "You should buy that one. That's the one you want." He gestures again toward Farrah.

I watch the clerk's face and worry that he's losing patience with us. Why can't Papi see that he doesn't care which poster I buy? The hand resting on my shoulder starts to feel heavier, as my confusion turns into shame. It's not John Travolta that gives me away. Papi's shame betrays me. He works too hard to convince a stranger that I want Farrah Fawcett and not John Travolta. When we meet new people, Papi sounds like he's telling a joke no matter what he says. But now the laughter in his voice sounds desperate, like he's pleading my case in front of a judge. I resent Papi but feel sorry for him too. When he looks at me, his first American son, this country must feel more like an ending than a beginning to him. The clerk takes my five-dollar bill, and I leave the store with a rolled-up John Travolta poster. As we walk to the car, I switch it from hand to hand so I don't get it sweaty. I wonder if Papi forgot about his morir soñando or maybe he doesn't want one anymore.

What Papi doesn't realize is that I do want that Farrah Fawcett poster but not for the reasons that would make him happy. I want to be Farrah Fawcett. I want to be Farrah Fawcett and I want to marry Lee Majors. Not Colonel Steve Austin from *Six Million Dollar Man* but the younger Lee Majors, Heath Barkley from *Big Valley*. I watch *Big Valley* with Miracle. She likes it because it's set a long time ago, and I like it for the cowboys. The bastard son of Tom Barkley, Heath must fight his way into a family that rejects him. Nick, the oldest son, fights Heath that first night at the ranch. Jarrod, the sensible brother, offers him a few hundred dollars to disappear, but Heath stuffs the money into Jarrod's whiskey glass. Audra, the youngest, tries to seduce him in order to prove he's not really her brother, just a conman trying to steal Tom Barkley's name and fortune. But Miss Barbara Stanwyck, who plays Victoria—Tom Barkley's widow—calls Heath "son." I wonder how she can love her dead husband's bastard. Not even the ranch hands accept Heath. They refuse his orders and call him a mongrel whelped in a mining town.

Heath is short-tempered and broody. He wears tight pants and glowers all the time at something beyond the horizon, squinting as if the sun is in his eyes. It's like some terrible secret is always about to catch up with him. The picture on the TV screen is black and white, but everything about Heath is golden. At least that's how I imagine him. His tight golden jeans and his smooth, golden skin, golden hair parted on the left, where Mami tries to part and smooth my stubborn black hair. Hard hair like hers. I think about Heath squinting, deep in thought, troubled. I think about how his gun belt hangs lower on the right from the weight of his pistol, his golden hat tilted in the same direction. That's how I like to picture him. When *Big Valley* comes on I sit close to the TV screen to see into his eyes, hidden by the shadow of his cowboy hat, but Mami screams at me that I will go blind.

A picture of the Fawcett-Majors wedding I came across in a magazine mesmerizes me. I cut it out and hide it in a drawer of the white, pressed wood desk that Miracle and I share, the same drawer where I keep my *Charlie's Angels* trading cards. Lee's thick jaw, thick tie, thick shoulders, the baby fat on his face. Farrah's giant feral toothy smile, her feathered hair, the crooked geometry of her beauty. I feel like everything I want is contained in that one picture. The answer is there, right in front of my eyes, if only I could find the words to make sense of all the ways I want to be and to have and to not be in relation to that photo. I want to disappear in their white beauty. What do I call this feeling? I don't know a word that describes wanting something in a picture and you're not even sure what it is but being lost in the wanting is almost enough. Being lost in the wanting feels like being held by a stranger and leaving your body all at the same time. Empty and bursting and longing and nowhere all at once.

The Travolta poster goes up on the inside of our bedroom door immediately. My sister and Blanca act silly, squealing and pretend-fainting in front of the poster. They throw their bodies against Travolta creating a thud so loud I wonder if they smashed a hole in the door. Mami pokes her head into the bedroom.

"Niñas, por favor." She looks more tired than angry. "Miri, voy a El Gallo de Oro con tu papá. No le habran la puerta a nadie. Cuida a tu hermano."

Mami and Papi like El Gallo de Oro better than Winn Dixie or Piggly Wiggly. Mami knows the butcher by name and can bargain with him. Papi likes to smoke his cigar, order a cafecito from the café window, and make jokes with the other men waiting for their wives. Miracle and I hate it. The cages stuffed with guinea hens next to the entrance stink and I hate how scared they must be. Mami and Papi stop and talk to everyone as if they were best friends and it takes them forever to finish shopping, even if we only go in to pick up a loaf of Cuban bread and some Mazola oil. I am relieved to stay home with Miracle and Blanca. Besides, I know they must include me now that I gave Miracle her *Saturday Night Fever* poster.

As soon as we hear the front door close and the lock turn, Miracle and Blanca wonder aloud about Travolta's "manhood." They love to use words that they learn from Barbara Cartland novels. I hang around hoping to be included in their girl talk. Miracle asks me what I think about "manhood." Her invitation surprises me. I don't want to admit that I don't know what the word means and hear, "You're too young to know," for the millionth time.

"Let's play a game." Miracle grins. "I'll say a word and you say the first thing that comes to mind."

"Okay," I reply, nervous to prove myself. That smile means trouble for me. I know that on the inside, but I cannot resist the chance to belong. Belonging has to be earned.

"Manhood," my sister says, slowly this time, like we're on that gameshow *Password*. "Maaan-hood."

I draw a blank and panic. I know that the word is from Miracle's romance novels and, thinking I can fool them, confidently pronounce the most romantic word that comes to mind: "Beautiful."

Miracle and Blanca fall on the bed cackling; they repeat the words *beautiful manhood* but can barely get them out. The laughter continues for a long time until they begin coughing and their voices become hoarse. Humiliated, I wait silently, still hopeful I will be included. A knock at the front door interrupts their amusement. Rarely is it more than just the two of them—and me. But today the Berasategui sisters—Yvonne and Miozotis—arrive just in time to admire John Travolta and talk manhoods. The Berasateguis live two houses down from our duplex. They like to tell everyone that they are Basque. I don't know what that means but I do know they both have frizzy black hair that they keep tightly bunned and bobby-pinned. I like the older sister, Zoti, because she talks to me even though she is in junior high with my sister. During the summer, on days when I could find no one to play with me, Zoti let me sit on her porch. She recited the lyrics to "Dancing Queen" from her rocking chair so often that I learned it by heart. One time, she interrupted "Dancing Queen" to complain that Miracle and Blanca would be prettier if they didn't wear so much make-up. ("I don't care if you tell them I said that.") Another time, Zoti scrunched up her face when a couple of high school boys rolled up in a yellow Camaro, and the one in the passenger seat asked if we knew where Miracle lives. He had to yell because Zoti's old, short-legged dog Sam was barking like a killer on our side of the chain-link fence. I watched silently as Zoti mean-faced that boy and lied with a slow shake of her head. As they drove away, she sang Abba, just staring off into nowhere. The idea of high school boys chasing after my sister excited me, but I didn't understand why. The rest of the summer I wished for them to come back when Zoti wasn't around. To find my sister they needed to go through me. I never told Miri about the boys.

Yvonne is a year older than me but got left back a grade. She makes me nervous because she sees too much, mainly how other boys call me "pato" and "maricón" and how I don't do anything about it. Yvonne, who has the deepest dimples I've ever seen, laughs when she tells me the mean funny things her brother Junior says about me. Junior Berasategui rides a motorcycle, and he is much too old to care anything about me. He hangs out with boys from Coral Terrace because they look up to him. Already balding in his early twenties, Junior is unemployed and not much taller than me. I rarely see him without a helmet on his head. His patchy curls remind me of when I gave my old G.I. Joe doll a bath and a bunch of his hair fell out. Everyone says that Junior "fucks" the old woman who works at the 7-11 on Coral Way, the one who caught me stuffing candy into my shorts and told me never to come back or she was going to call the police. It's the first time I hear about two people I know in real life having sex. I don't like how this news makes me feel, like there's this whole other secret world and maybe I will never belong there either. Junior's best friend Frankie lives across the street from the Berasateguis. He and Junior like to ask me why I don't go with Yvonne or some other girl from my class. One time they asked why I don't go with Lovell West, the most albino white girl ever, who makes straight As and wears homemade clothes and a thin silver cross around her neck. I didn't want to say anything mean about Lovell, but when I replied that she's too conceited they cracked up laughing. Another time Junior told me I couldn't touch my knuckles to my shoulders. *Yes I can*, I insisted, raising my knuckles up to my shoulders, the palms of my hands facing out. Everyone laughed and pointed. *You're such a faggot*, Junior said. He and Frankie riled up the boys on our block to jump me. Perched on his motorcycle, Junior screamed at me: *Be a man! Fight back!* I didn't fight back. *Look at his eyes*, he laughed. *Yeah, look at his eyes*, Frankie repeated.

I imagine myself stone-faced and wonder what exactly my eyes tell when I get kicked and punched. My size does not protect me. I am always the biggest boy in my class yet that only makes me the biggest target. When I walk by a pack of boys, a part of me senses their hackles going up. Even if I do not fight back, my size makes me a trophy in their eyes. "Grande por gusto," they call me. Big for nothing.

But today it's the Berasategui sisters making an unexpected visit. Zoti is selling Avon for her mom and Yvonne tags along. Miracle tells the sisters they should wait for Mami to return. She invites them to our room to show off her new John Travolta poster. Really they just want to talk about manhoods, except now they say "dicks." Each one of them claims to be a bigger expert than the next. No one notices me, which makes me both happy and nervous. Miracle is the authority on the different kinds of dick. Black dicks are long and thick; white dicks are thin little library pencils; Chinese dicks are small and stubby; Cuban dicks are average length and thick. They all laugh. Something inside me shudders when I hear my sister mention "Chinese dicks." Who does she mean? We call Mami a crazy Chinese sometimes, even though she gets angry. We hardly ever say "Filipina." I don't think of Miri as part Filipina, but I feel that way. A part but also apart. Mixed up. A bunch of parts that don't add up, which really is closer to being nothing than being something. Not chino but *chino*, the way Papi says it like a punchline when he laughs telling stories about Mami's father who chose not to come to Los Estados Unidos. None of Mami's family came. He wants us to be in on the joke like Mami's blood isn't part of who we are too. Maybe I feel this way because I'm more Mami's son the way Miri is more Papi's daughter. She's even dark like he is. There are sides. Always there have to be sides.

I think I am a fly on the wall until Zoti—who never has been cruel to me—asks, "What kind of dick do you have, Hiram?"

She smiles but it's not a smile I've seen before. Not from her at least. She's still Miozotis Berasategui but she's not the same Zoti from the summer. Now she's a stranger from my sister's school, and suddenly I know from the way her whole face grins at me—how even her chin held high is a kind of grin—that we will never again spend an afternoon together, her on her rocking chair reciting Abba songs like they are poems from her diary and Sam the mean black dog sniffing the grass and pissing and me with my legs dangling from the tall, covered porch wondering why old dog piss cooked into dried up lawns smells a certain way and thinking how funny it is not feeling even a little scared and doesn't the rain ever wash the piss smell away.

I'm scared now. What am I supposed to say? I do not answer Zoti's question but Miri does.

"Hiram has a Chinese dick."

I turn my head to meet Miri's eyes. She looks so happy. Is it Zoti or Yvonne who screams *GROSS*?

"I'll show you," Miracle announces.

Before I know what is happening, Miracle and Blanca tackle me to the ground. Blanca straddles me, tightening her knees around the outside of my thighs while Miracle holds my arms. I wrestle with Miracle but can't free myself. Blanca tries to steady herself in order to unbutton my jeans but I kick and buck as hard as I can. She pulls on my jeans. One of my hands is close to Miracle's hair and I grab it. I clench my fist and determine not to let go. My sister does not surrender. I feel hands on my ankles but can't be sure whose they are. Blanca continues to pull at my pants until they give, and then my underwear, and then I am exposed. I close my eyes and pull as hard as I can on Miracle's hair.

"Blanca, help me!"

They work to disentangle my fingers from her hair while still pinning me to the floor. But I cannot open my fingers even if I try. The rage makes my ears burn. My whole head feels hot. I am a wild animal fighting for my life. I will tear the hair from her head before letting go. My chest heaves and tears run down the sides of my face. After several minutes, Miracle and Blanca manage to free her hair. I feel my limbs released, and I grab at my underwear, then my jeans. My hands tremble so hard I struggle to zipper and button my jeans. I brace for another assault but see that my attackers have retreated. My eyes search the room. I remain cautious. I go into the living room and realize that Miracle and Blanca have vanished. The Berasategui sisters too. I turn the bolt on the front door, then check the back door to make sure it's locked. I return to the living room to sit on the arm of the sofa with my eyes on the front door, watching and listening for danger, except all I can hear is my own breathing. Finally, someone tries to turn the doorknob. Then more waiting.

Miracle returns with our elderly landlord, Mr. Victor, to let her and Blanca back inside. He smiles when he spots me seething, my jaw clenched so hard I cannot speak. What does he see? A bad-tempered child prone to rages—un malcriado. Miracle and Blanca thank Mr. Victor, close the door, and resume their gossiping, as if nothing happened. Instinctively I understand the unspoken contract between us. Our parents tire of our battles, and I tire of disgracing them by not acting right for a boy. As I bury another secret inside of me, shame washes away any trace of rage. On top of crying, I had pulled Miracle's hair. Only girls fight that way. Only girls cry. A few seconds ago, my rage felt enormous and powerful, but now it floats away like a feather, carried by the whispers and titters of Miracle and Blanca. The shame has a heaviness to it though, like the weight of my father's hand on my shoulder when I bought the John Travolta poster. It is Sunday. I wonder what Yvonne will say at school the next morning. The worry keeps me up.

"Mami and Papi paid somebody to come beat you up and make you a man," Miracle prattles on. It is late. Our bodies meet in the sunken groove at the middle of the bed we have shared almost all my life. "You better fight back or they will find out you're a maricón. It's a test."

I should know not to believe her lies but some part of me always does. The truth in her lies keeps me awake long after Miracle gets too sleepy to continue her torment.

"It's your turn," she says. "You hold me now."

We shift positions and I spoon her.

SPECIAL FEATURE:

Who doesn't love a good creative prompt? For those of us who are writers, prompts (and themed calls for submissions) can cultivate general creativity, provide a place to begin a narrative, and help strengthen unfocused prose. Our third annual special feature (following Queer Flash Science Fiction in Issue #27 and Black & White Neurodivergent Artwork in Issue #28) was crafted to be more open-ended than its predecessors. What would "____ Punk" mean to our submitters? We hereby present five pieces that we found to be excellent examples of flash creative nonfiction:

THE GOOD BANDS ARE ON SKATE VIDEO SOUNDTRACKS

LAUREN LAVÍN

Jake moves to our block with his stuttering kickflips in sixth grade. He's tall and has the same name as one of the Animorphs so he's perfect in my eyes. Later I try to skate for his attention but I can't stomach the way the board rolls out from under me, the imbalance, so I start learning guitar because he has one. Soon I'm writing my own songs, and I don't mind when he asks me to teach him how to play his beautiful girlfriend's favorites. In eighth grade he introduces me to some high school guys he skates with. *They're coming over to play guitar so I think you should come* he says. *I feel like you and Frank will fall madly in love.* I wear a skirt I made and an Alkaline Trio shirt I cut up and stitched tight over to Jake's house, where Frank with long black hair is noodling on a guitar and his friend Bob with long blonde hair picks quietly and doesn't look up much. I think Bob is cute but mostly I'm aware of Jake's bed and comforter under my legs. By the time I decide Jake is just a boring guy with too comfortable a home life, he's already moved to a different state. But I still wear shoes you're supposed to skate in.

Years later, I'm nineteen and working at Jamba Juice with Alex, one of the sweet punk guys I'd met slamming around at shows or smoking Black & Mild spliffs in the creek during summer breaks. He skates, too, in sharp, fierce movements that make me think *shark*. One night after we close he takes me to a party where I see Bob, from Jake's room. Bob stares with pale blue eyes while I play and sing old punk songs we both like on some guitar. The first time we break up, I tell him *it's like a lightbulb that just won't turn on* and I don't know why I'm only lit up about him part-time. He's lit up like crazy about me, but he's angry too, bitter that he fucked up his knee and can't skate anymore. He hooks up with a friend of his who has a perfect body, and I forget all the times Bob made me feel beautiful, and I know he'll get back with me if I want to because he's still heartbroken, so on Halloween I get him back. I find the girl's Tumblr where she writes about how upset she is that Bob chose me instead of her again, and I think *good.*

Alex brings Tony, who skates with something like grace and earnest in his figure, to a party at Kate's and my apartment. Tony laughs loud and has a killer smile, big straight white teeth. I'm drunk when he introduces himself and I howl *Wow, you have great teeth!* Kate thinks he's hot, so I don't examine my curiosity about him, and I don't know that this same party is his first attempt to come out from a long period of isolation following an army stint in Afghanistan. As the party winds down and shapes start smearing, Tony and Alex go fucking around in the skatepark across the street. Tony stumbles, eats shit, and breaks off his two front teeth in the bowl. I learn about it from a picture I'm tagged in the next day and I'm horrified, like I cursed his teeth. Bob or Alex reassures me it's fine, *he's got that army insurance.*

Bob connects me with his best friend Cory, who also skates, because we both write. I ask Cory if Bob will like the bootleg Photosynthesis and Mindfield DVDs I found for his birthday, and he says *he'll like anything you get him.* I start seeing Cory around the community college campus, and I like his cold indifference and the high contrast thrown in my face when it suddenly evaporates into interest, when the beetle black eyes stay a little too long on mine. Our emails get lengthier and our swapped stories get more sexual and less fictional. I romanticize his drug addictions and his love for the *clack-clack* of wheels over asphalt equally, imagining them as high towers that keep him ideologically and creatively pure, untouchable, in a way that feeds my fearful need to be in constant pursuit of, rather than sitting in one place with, a person.

Bob's ever-increasing rage toward me is probably driven by my growing indifference. I'm sick of him calling me a bitch when we fight and the lightbulb shuts off when, in Cory's backyard, he tells a story about a girl they know who *let a bunch of guys run a train on her* and I'm like *Maybe she had a great time, what's the problem?* I feel for Cory's eyes with my periphery as Bob explains, *A lock that opens for any key is a shitty lock. But a key that can open any lock...* We break up for good. Tony and I spend more time together and there are a few grayed-out attempts to connect bodies, but it rubs me wrong, to be an expected thing, and anyway Cory and I are still talking, he's telling me I'd make a good wife for him and asks me to meet him in Vegas and get married, and I don't know if I'm scared to be a fool when it turns out he doesn't mean it, or if my own disbelief is enough to make any *us* unreal, but for a decade he cycles in and out of me, says *I love you*, disappears and reappears. The words hurt and confuse, and even though I want to, I never say them back because, in some creatively pure, untouchable way, I feel ran-through.

NOT PUNK ENOUGH; SKA PUNK ENOUGH

JOHN KIM

WHEN WE GOT TO THE SHOW, I saw a kid in the parking lot smoking a cigarette while popping the deck of his skateboard. Didn't he know that the straightedge crew had just sent Todd to the ER last month? Messing up his face, breaking his ribs? Maybe the kid didn't know. Or maybe he was keeping his skateboard close in case he needed to take a swing at someone in self-defense.

This was Dayton in the mid-'90s. The straightedge crew wore varsity jackets and would kick your ass if you had a beer or a cigarette. I went to punk shows to escape this kind of bullshit. I could get beat up for no reason staying at home. I could get beat up by an asshole in a varsity jacket back at high school.

I came to punk the way a lot of Asian Americans growing up in the Midwest in the '90s did. New Wave was the first music that connected to the alienation I felt growing up in a white community. But while New Order, Erasure, and The Cure spoke to my loneliness, none of them could touch my anger and angst.

Then came grunge. I can still remember the MTV premiere for "Smells Like Teen Spirit" in eighth grade. At the end of the video two Asian kids help Kurt smash his guitar. Outside of the token Asian Americans on *The Real World*, they were the only Asian Americans on MTV that decade, and they were going harder than anyone else. They were my fucking heroes. I wanted to move to Seattle and become friends with them.

Nirvana was my special secret favorite band for about two months until they became everyone's favorite band. I couldn't listen to the same music as the people who were making my life miserable. I had to find something harder and angrier—less mopey, more middle fingers.

Enter punk. When Kurt Cobain died, I didn't care. He was a sellout. Nirvana sucked. I was listening to Rancid and the Ramones. There were punk rock kids in my grade, but I wasn't punk enough for them. They pretended they didn't know me at shows. Two of them did the post-dismissal show for our school's radio station. Every Friday they played "The Brews" by NOFX. One Friday when they hadn't played it yet, I called in to request it. They got excited and asked who was calling. When I said my name they said, "Oh," and hung up.

Getting into Rancid led me to Operation Ivy, which opened a whole new world of music to me: ska punk. That's how I found out that the frontperson of one of the seminal ska punk bands was Korean.

What would my life be if Ian McKaye was Korean? I didn't have Ian McKaye, but I did have Mike Park of Skankin' Pickle.

At a time when, outside of martial arts, the only visible Asian American in the entertainment industry was Margaret Cho, hearing Mike Park sing "Onyonghasayo" for Skankin' Pickle was a revelation. The lyrics were basic phrases in Korean that a Korean American child might know, sung in Mike's shitty American-born Korean accent. A rough translation of the opening lines: "Hello. Goodbye. I suck at speaking Korean." Listening to that song filled me with joy. Finally, a band and a scene that saw me and made a space for me.

I admit that my favorite band in high school was named after a dancing condiment. All through college I had a silk-screened Skankin' Pickle patch—a smiling cartoon pickle wearing sunglasses and gloves—safety-pinned to my canvas knapsack. I thought I looked tough and cool like the punks with their Black Flag and Bad Religion patches. I can see now that I was asking far too much of those safety pins.

But nobody gets into ska punk because it's cool. Two of the greatest ska punk bands—Operation Ivy and Slapstick—broke up after only a few years. Then their members went on to start much cooler punk bands. Rancid, Schlong ("Punk Side Story," anyone?), Alkaline Trio, The Lawrence Arms, among others. They got out.

Most punk rockers think that ska punk sucks—just ask Propaghandi who penned the oft-covered song "Ska Sucks." Ska traditionalists—like mods and skinheads—think ska punk is an abomination.

I moved to New York for college and went to all the ska shows that I could. At the traditional ska shows there was a group of skinheads who seemingly only came to beat people up. They weren't white power skinheads, but they all wore Fred Perry shirts and bomber jackets with American flag patches on them. As I kept my distance, I questioned if I was part of the America that they felt the flag represented. I never got close enough to ask. To me, they were just like the straightedge clowns that I'd left behind in Dayton only wearing a different uniform.

Ska punk is for the unloved and unwanted. The rejects. The lower case "m" misfits. Not punk enough to fuck someone up in the pit. Band geeks with an edge. All we wanted was a place to listen to music and dance without getting beat up. I never saw a militant straightedge kid or a skinhead at a ska punk show. We had a pit, but everyone skanked in the pit together.

I'm not saying that nobody ever got hurt at a ska punk show. I'm sure it's happened, but I can say with 100% certainty and with doing no research whatsoever that there has never been a neo-Nazi ska punk band. That kind of hatred and violence just isn't part of the genre. Our classic anthem has the lyrics, "Unity! As one we stand together!" not, "I get pissed, destroy!"

When I first discovered Nirvana, I wanted a band that was only for me. But what I found in ska punk was a music that invited everyone in to join the party.

GUTTER PUNK

MOLLY ANNE BLUMHOEFER

Pretty and I swigged whiskey with two Guadalupe Street dragworms midday on the banks of Waller Creek in Austin. One worm was an old snaky looking punk in his 40s; the other, his sidekick, a wingnut grunger in his 20s. Pretty mentioned to them that we were heading to San Fran. I whispered, "Are you sure? I don't really like California punks."

Pretty responded loudly, "Haight has tons of pretty punks like you. You'll fit in. You're quiet." That was generally true, but he meant that Haight Street crawled with runaways. He smiled vulgarly at no one, at himself. He also idolized the San Francisco Scum Fucks, a self-proclaimed infamous gutter punk crew.

I had never been to California, but I'd met some SFSFs in Minneapolis. Most gutter punks in the nineties were kind-hearted inside their armors of tattoos, band patches, butt flaps, and sharp accessories; but the SFSFs I met one summer by the tracks were something brutal, pure trauma. They wore scars on scars—grime covered like the rest of us—but violence lived beneath SFSFs and other carvings in their foreheads, knuckles, and necks. Their malevolence oozed onto half-broken kids like me, as if to break us fully. At age thirteen I found myself in an abandoned warehouse with a few SFSFs and one of their notorious members smeared violence into my body and then called me ugly for weeks until he disappeared.

I couldn't talk about what happened in the warehouse. Even though it had been more than a year; it was trapped in my bones, decades from my mouth.

The old snaky punk told us about a train line near Houston that went to California and asked if he and his wingnut could join us. Pretty accepted, reasoning that it would be safer. I didn't agree but kept my quiet.

Early the next morning, we started from Austin for the train yard. I stood solo beside the highway with my thumb out. When someone stopped, the guys popped out from beneath an underpass or ditch; the car would speed away as Pretty yelled, "You fuckin' pervert!" The old punk shook his head at me. His wingnut cackled. We finally got lucky after walking hours into shin splints and dehydration.

A faded blue pickup pulled over. I opened the passenger door. The driver looked the same age as Pretty, early twenties. His face was scruffy. His light brown hair stuck out from beneath a ragged baseball cap. He wore a sleeveless red t-shirt that was two-toned from his sweaty chest, cut so low around his arms that I could see his glistening pit hair and a few ribs— a common nineties look. His jeans showed a day's work. He gently asked where I was headed and why I was out there by myself. I was smitten.

Everything about him was prettier than Pretty, who I had outgrown in a mere day. I no longer cared about his deep-set blue eyes, brawny physique, and other attributes that earned him his nickname. I contemplated shouting, "Go! Hurry! Please go!" Instead, I held my bait position and threw my bag and body into the front seat while the guys crawled into the bed.

He wasn't pleased but reacted rather kindly, yelled out the window, "Just don't fucking do anything stupid." Then he turned towards me sternly, "You get in the back with them."

The wind threw sand into my eyes and further dried my sunbaked face. I held my hood down as far as possible; I focused on large lug nuts and bolts dancing inside the rusted grooves of the truck bed. The two-hour stretch felt like an entire day.

He dropped us off in downtown Houston, where we spanged a few bucks and a banana from passersby. With a few hours of daylight left, we went back to the highway and continued for the train yard.

We slept on a grassy area, under the yellow highway lights, inches from the shoulder. I pulled the hood of my mummy bag around my head tightly. I couldn't stop thinking about what three grown men could do to a sleeping girl.

I kept my eyes open for as long as possible. My lids ached as I watched a scorpion crawl along the road, surprised to see one in the desert's chilly weather. It was light brown with golden appendages, like the shades of the prettier-than-Pretty man's hair who had driven us to Houston. I imagined that we were together on the hood of his faded truck, our knees pointed at the moon, eating fast food from paper bags and drinking cans of beer. We mapped the stars, Ursa Major and Orion. We discussed our future, kids and all. A trashy lullaby.

I slept until moments before dawn and quickly released myself from the grips of the mummy bag. I looked around for snakes and scorpions that bled from my sleep. We gathered our stuff under the cracking darkness. The landscape looked fake, but intentional, like a large oil painting in a museum. Barely visible lines drawn by the fields and highway merged into the peeking horizon.

The dewed ground sparkled as thick golden sunbeams grew fast across the earth, fueling an awesome sense of resurrection, or something like epiphany. I shook moisture from my belongings and talked to Pretty about scorpions, about their many colors that I had never known.

He looked away from me and told me under his breath to quit acting like a kid. He was paranoid that the guys might suspect I was a minor. A terrifying realization overcame me: Pretty is dumb. I'm not safe. I held back tears and despite my life almost unquietly announced, I am a kid.

HOMOCORE RISING

RICHARD LORANGER

I WAS DRAWN TO PUNK in the early '80s by its alertness and attitude, its pushback against ideological monoliths and the corporate steamroller. I could feel it. Gay culture of the era, not so much. When I moved from Michigan to San Francisco, I was excited to find my place in it, but despite its flamboyance and rule-breaking lifestyle, there really wasn't one for a grungy anti-capitalist in what seemed like an almost desperate conformity to limited social roles. Then in 1988, SF-based *Homocore Magazine* reared its mohawked head as the gay punk scene began to bloom there and in Chicago, Toronto, Minneapolis, then everywhere. Along with countless marginalized queers around the world, I was beyond thrilled. It was a reason to dance, and that's exactly what we did.

I started contributing to *Homocore* and helping with their music shows, which were the slamming heart of the movement. These weren't your standard show-up-and-flail hardcore events by any means. They were all-ages, all-genders, all-persuasions (yes even straight-friendly), filled with performance, information booths, drag wardrobes, makeup tables (I'd bring my 50 colors of nail polish), and all sorts of tomfoolery and love. And all kinds of music—yeah, punk, which meant whatever-we-fucking-wanted-to-play music of freedom, anger, and smashing taboos. The shows featured acts like the Popstitutes, Comrades in Arms, Sabot, X-Tal, Gwenfish & Bucket, and Valerie, culminating in the harder sounds of MDC, Blue Vulva Underground, Kamala and the Karnivores, and on three occasions, Fugazi. They felt like celebrations.

I emceed several of them including the Fugazi triptych, which attracted a broader music audience with whom we were overjoyed to share our ardent new homo-culture. I'll use them to give you a closer peek as well. The first was at the Women's Building in 1989 and beyond Fugazi the divertissement included Swollen Boss Toad, Daisy Anarchy, a gaggle of rad poets, and Box Car Darla, all for a crowd of about 600. It started with an unannounced piece by the High Risk Group, a postmodern dance/theater troupe that I also worked with. We performed edgy vignettes all through the audience; in one I was required to eat raw meat until I choked to death. When I jumped on stage to officially kick off the show, I still had chunks of tenderloin stuck to my shirt. The kids those days.

The 1990 show took place in a large hall with bleachers at the old SF Russian Center, packed with about 1,500 people. The place was ancient and so Russian that, despite the Soviet Union dissolving pretty much that very minute, the stage was adorned with a U.S. flag and a pre-Soviet Russian flag on either side. This show was the most extravagant of them all. Fugazi headlined with Beat Happening but only after three hours of bands, performance art, films, puppets, ranting, how-to demonstrations, and general chaos. One skit that seared itself into my memory was a "dance" piece by the Popstitutes in which a seven-foot-tall queer boy dressed as the Statue of Liberty bullwhipped a short, stout drag Uncle Sam all over the stage to electronic music. Ahem. As Fugazi was finally about to go on, I stepped out to intro them with a rant I'd written a couple of years before for Big Black, basically questioning every motive that anyone might have for being there. Some guy in the bleachers didn't like being questioned so he ripped a fire extinguisher off the wall and sprayed it at the stage, filling the poorly ventilated and overcrowded auditorium with tiny particles that absorbed oxygen. The guy was ejected (literally down the front steps) by a bunch of pissed-off punks, and everyone had to wait outside for forty-five minutes until it was safe to finish the show. Still Fugazi banged it out and everyone who hung around went home pleased and filled with protestant vigor.

Amazingly, Fugazi returned the next year, and even more amazingly, *Homocore* managed to secure the marble-domed amphitheater atop the Scottish Rite Masonic Center in Oakland. This show was pared down and more "orderly" than the previous. For one thing, there were just two opening acts, Nation of Ulysses and Her Majesty the Baby. For another, everyone was seated—in tiers of red velvet. And I was set on bringing people together just a titch better than last time.

When the hall was mostly filled with the 2,000 or so attendees, I had a sudden whim and sprang up to welcome everyone. I was like, "Wow, look at this room!" Most everyone was talking about it and digging it. "And that dome," I said. "The acoustics in here are crazy." They were. "Why don't we make some noise and see how it sounds?" This crowd make noise? They started yelling immediately. "That's right, let's get a little aggression out," I suggested. "How about for a minute, everybody yell about something that's pissing you off." An impressive cacophony swelled, then morphed into applause. "That was so cool," I went on. "Let's try another." This time I suggested that everyone sing a different song at once. Wasn't sure if it would work but I started in with a droll version of "Sing a Song" by The Carpenters. Maybe they wanted to drown me out or maybe they liked the idea; whichever the case, they all started singing and a different beautiful cacophony was born, leaving everyone quite amused. "All right," I said, "how about one more. This place is like a huge soundbox and I bet it has a harmonic tone that'll really reverberate if we can find it. Let's try. Everyone make a tone and shift it around to see if we can find the harmonic of the room." And they did. And they found it. And we all stood there for who knows how long mesmerized by that tone thrumming and reverbing and throbbing through the space, through everything, through our nerves and minds.

GIRL'S LULLABY

ANGELICA WHITEHORNE

"If I know one thing is that I cannot just be a peach." — Bon Iver

our girlish tones / out of tune / squealing over stereo / not nice / not neat /
pink hair streak / so teen / my midriff showing / your ripped jeans, a
smiley face where the skin slipped through, hand-drawn in blue ink /
and if our girlhood was a lullaby it was off-key / wrapped in
sugar beds all our lives / and still our candy mouths were
smoking underneath / knowing something was coming /
always on guard / keeping our bodies on our mind /
our minds in our bodies / and both out of basements / which
was a harmony of sorts / was a punk performance / you could hear
our legs scream lead. / me and my best friend then / slow bobbed to
a sound so loud it hurt / but not worse than running from the
things / behind us / and at our sides / grab and release /
flocks of fish / class in session / ring the bell / some will be lost /
that's hunger / that's the open sea / that's this concert that your
parents hand delivered us to / hands in prayer behind their backs /
knowing that crowds eat / but knowing also that girls have feet /
and will go / despite their flesh stinking of rose water / and baby powder /
and how to some that innocence / means wanting / means its time to feed /
some will be lost—so stay together! / most sharks can't fit two in between their
teeth / which means logistically / some girls are bound to survive. / and we were giiiirls /
and we were cool / almost always / but I remember on that day / in that mess
of strangers how / your fist did find my fist and wrap it / our lips lathered in
bubblegum hibiscus whatever / our eyeliner ready / to drip in gothic greeting
to the night. / girlhood: a lullaby of a banshee / of a flock of crows / of a tire screech,

the girls in the front row howled / and we, in back yodeled replies of swords /
and soil / making sense of no sense / of violence / spit on my palm / make this pact /
pathogens and exclamations / deep in this crowd / no return / elbows and asses
banging into elbows / and asses / moments are music are moments lasting. /
us hoping their instruments would splinter / if they played too close to us /
us becoming gleaming / teaming breakthroughs / unmelodious midwives /
patching with poultice the holes the world had / yet to make / but at least
we were free / to bleed / floor of broken glass / scratching our way forward,
all drum / all that / all the things we would grow into below us /
us above it all / in the realm where the music lives /
where the prayers are answered / where the girls
always make it home after the set / ends.

YOU DON'T SAY

Timothy Nolan

what I am & expect me to remain silent
but I'll say what I am & say it again
as you outlaw the saying of it.

You pin another bull's eye
on my swishing tail & dredge
up those terrible old tropes.

My heart is a rugged peak
reflected in a glass-top lake
set afire by the rising sun.

Your throat gags on each
transgression conjured up
& served in abundance.

I was the child who learned
what I was & what I wanted
straight from a bully's mouth.

Let every scapegoat teach this:
the *shielded* child learns to count
high enough to fly   far, far from home.

FACING IT

Jack Bordnick

mixed media
8" × 10"

STORM ON THE HORIZON

Robert Palmer

oil on linen
48" × 48"

SPEAKING WITH THE AUTHOR OF *RADIANT FUGITIVES*

Nawaaz Ahmed

WINNER, 2022 GINA BERRIAULT AWARD

14H: You've mentioned that this book took upwards of a decade to complete. What advice do you have for those writers who like to take their time in a world that is biased towards output and productivity?

NA: *Radiant Fugitives* did take ten years from the time I started the first draft to the time I handed in the final draft to my editor. There were definitely moments during those ten years when I convinced myself I was done, especially after my second and fourth drafts. Looking back, I knew even then that the novel wasn't there yet, there were things I knew I hadn't gotten right. I just wanted to be done, to have the book out for the reasons you mentioned. I was also afraid the book would come out too late and lose its relevance once the Obama presidency ended. But I couldn't let the book go out into the world knowing that it didn't quite capture my vision for it, especially when I also thought I knew what I needed to do to fix it.

Were the ten years worth it? I couldn't have written this novel, as it stands in its final form, without having gone through the journey. My one piece of advice is to trust your instinct if it says your work isn't done, but also make sure you're not holding on to it only because you're afraid to let it go or afraid of how it will be received. The book will never be fully done, and you send out the book you can live with.

14H: As writers, titling can often be a difficult thing for us to do. There's an interesting tension going on within the title, *Radiant Fugitives*, which seems to mirror or amplify the many tensions at play in the work. The word "radiant" has positive connotations, even spiritual ones; it's a word often associated, at least in western literature, with the heavens. Fugitives, on the other hand, can carry with it an element of danger, of trying to flee from something, or of lacking a static home. Can you speak more to how you arrived at this title, and how you see it as an entry point to your novel?

NA: I have to admit that *Radiant Fugitives* isn't the original title of the book and came pretty late in the process, at a suggestion from my editor, Dan Smetanka, from a line at the end of the novel. (Thank you, Dan!) The previous title (I'm not going to say what it is!) did guide me through the various early drafts, but I think by the time the book was done, it subtracted from the book, emphasizing one reading. Similarly, I had two epigraphs (one quote from the Quran and the other from Keats) throughout the many years I worked on the book, which I dropped from the final version because they were no longer needed—the book was already doing their work, which is to capture the tensions you've noted, between the heavenly and the worldly, the predetermined and the sought out, the beauty promised by paradise and the beauty of the earth, the costs extracted by each. While looking for alternate titles, *Radiant Fugitives* stood out because it too captured the same tensions, but through a dramatic image, and a question rather than a statement: the characters in my novel are fugitives, seeking new loves, new homes, new worlds, new ways of being, but are they radiant because of something intrinsic to them or are they reflecting the light they're fleeing from or journeying towards?

14H: Poetry, particularly the works of John Keats, shows up frequently throughout the book, especially as a point of bonding between many of the characters, namely in the relationship between sisters Seema and Tahera, but also with the two sisters and their father. Why did you choose Keats, of all poets, to serve as this through-line of communication between these family members so unable to speak honestly with one another?

NA: I started out writing poetry before I turned to fiction. I love the ways poetry seeks to express what prose cannot quite capture, through allusion, evasion, omission, association, juxtaposition, ambiguity, polysemy, etc. These techniques create spaces for the reader to inhabit and make their own, and to allow for multiple and even contradictory interpretations to exist simultaneously, and when I set out to write my novel, I wanted it to function in a similar manner, knowing that what I wanted to write about (love and faith and the meaning of life!) was too vast and too splintered to be tackled directly. So poetry was on my mind from the very start, but soon it also became the subject of the novel as well. I was searching for secular alternatives to god, religion, and faith that the characters could explore, and beauty, art, and love seemed to me the replacements the modern world has come up with so far, with poetry as their literary medium. It seemed appropriate to probe the different ways we seek meaning through religious and poetic texts, and the ways we share the resulting knowledge through reference to them.

Growing up in India, most of the poetry I studied in my Anglo-Indian school was British Romantic poetry, a relic of India's colonial past. My initial idea was to incorporate as much of it as seemed relevant, without restricting myself to any particular poet. It became pretty evident very soon that I'd have to be more specific if I wanted to make progress—there was simply too much poetry to choose from. I settled on Wordsworth and Keats, for their contrasts. Wordsworth advocated for poetry as "emotion recollected in tranquility" while Keats's poetry eschewed tranquility for angst and passion. Tahera's approach to both faith and life is inherently Keatsian, and I made her more remote father an admirer of Wordsworth, which spoke to their differences.

14H: The rich characterization in your writing really resonated with me. We live in a time of intense polarity and othering, and there feels like a deep desire for many of us, especially folks who are marginalized in some way, to be seen as the sum of their parts, rather than pigeon-holed or stereotyped. I appreciated your complex rendering of Tahera and Seema.

Though they are deeply different ideologically, both felt dynamic on the page; you didn't shy away from showing them in their ugliest moments, but they were easy to empathize with because of how effectively you represented them. Can you speak to how you developed these nuanced characters and their relationships, both with each other and with others in the book?

NA: I think the biggest factor that opened up the novel and its characters to me was my choice to have the novel narrated by Seema's just-born baby. Having a clear narrator allowed me, as the writer, sufficient distance from my characters. The sisters are very different ideologically, as you note, and in initial drafts I found my own ideological hangups getting in the way of treating both characters fairly. I was judging them, especially Tahera, and it was hard to keep my judgements from coloring how the characters acted and responded to each other. But the baby narrator is neutral, learning about the events that led to his mother's death along with the reader, and being reminded constantly to see the characters through his non-judgmental eyes kept me from imposing my authorial valuations on them, or to recognize those instances when I was failing them.

The device of the baby narrator also permitted me to play with both point of view and distance. The baby narrator inhabits the consciousness of all the characters, switching between their points of view at will, sometimes within the same scene, and he can adopt both a close-third as well as step back to comment on the events directly, a form of magical omniscience. So we get to see some critical events from multiple points of view, receiving these views on equal footing, and since the baby's commentary is usually sympathetic, the characters are often softened even at their ugliest moments.

The other factors, I think, are time and revision. Living with these characters for ten years, through multiple drafts, did help me gain insight into them. Also, something I learned from a wonderful teacher (Kevin McIlvoy, whose novel writing workshop I took early in the process) was a guide through the entire process of revision: everything a character does, he said, including moving a pencil, must have an outcome that is felt later in the book. An important aspect of revision is to identify these outcomes and make them count. This required me to be on the lookout for all the ways, big and small, that the words and actions of one character could affect the others.

14H: Being that we are a journal run by graduate students working towards their MAs and MFAs, I think I speak for both myself and my peers when saying there's often a lot of anxiety and trepidation about life after school. So I'm wondering, did the MFA assist you in transitioning from the tech sector into a writing life? Or did you already have a strong writing practice that your MFA program served to solidify?

NA: I did have a writing practice before my MFA, but that was only for the year prior, and the two years of my program did help to establish it more firmly. But I think it wasn't until I committed to my novel that I approached my practice with enthusiasm—it was exciting to keep returning to the project and adding to it daily. Working on short stories did not give me that same thrill, perhaps because I was always aware of the looming end and the concomitant judgment soon to be made.

I get the trepidation about life after school—writing has to be more self-driven, there's no structure, there are no deadlines, you have to carve out time and energy in the midst of living and making a living, and after all that you also fear that you're not very good and that there maybe no one waiting to read what you've written. I think it helps to be working on something that feels like it has to be written, and that there's no one else beside you to do it. Identifying your true subject is half the battle; committing to it is the other half. And hopefully the program has, at the very least, provided its students with a community to reassure them of the value of their writing and with readers eager to read their work.

14H: Finally, I always like to ask: what have you read lately that has bowled you over or blown you away?

NA: Since my book came out I've been finding it hard to get into fiction and have been reading more nonfiction and computer science articles. I'm hoping that will change soon. But a couple of novels have given me immense pleasure, for the wonderful ways they blend fiction and nonfiction. In Nicholson Baker's *The Mezzanine*, an escalator ride made me want to look more carefully at the world again, and Italo Calvino's *Cosmicomics* is a delightful reimagining of space, time, and the origins of life.

حنين

HANEEN

Jennifer Gauthier

A MAN, our man, his blue-gray nylon duffel bag heavy with herbs, eggplant, early-summer fruit, cardamom coffee, and date cookies for his granddaughter, turns onto Maarouf El Rassafi Street. With each vigorous step, the well-worn rubber soles of his beige canvas shoes crush bright fallen poinciana blossoms, streaking the sidewalk with red-orange smudges.

To his right, the water treatment facility, a humming industrial slab. To his left, behind concrete walls, through the bougainvillea, morning glories, and palm fronds, he sees a section of terracotta roof; then, a tall, skinny window with cobalt shutters; then, a dark wooden trellis.

Waving to the cluster of doormen sitting together on plastic chairs, he says, *Salaam aleykoum.* The men smile and wave to him: *Aleykoum elsalaam wa rahmat Allah wa barakatoh.* One of them puts his hand over his heart and nods; our man responds in kind.

Stepping over and around familiar tree-root ruptures in the sun-dappled pavement, he hears the thsk thsk thsk of a water sprinkler. From underneath locked double doors, a thin trickle of water streams down a short driveway into the street. Passing by, he inhales slowly, savoring the smell of freshly cut grass, thickly sweet gardenia, zesty cypress.

Toward the end of Maarouf El Rassafi, azalea branches, exhausted from weeks of rampant blooming, droop over the graffiti-smeared wall of the Franciscan school, closed for the summer.

He used to take the long way home from the *souk* just to walk down this street.

He doesn't walk here anymore.

احمد السيد محمد ابوزيد / 1944–2019

A BONEYARD OF FLESH// POST-WAR TRAUMA

Nnadi Samuel

WINNER, 2023 STACY DORIS MEMORIAL POETRY AWARD

"my joy is a dead language"—KHALYPSO

1.
yet, a nameless gravestone rolled between cold war & now.
a maddened apparition, manifesting from the boys' quarter of my pain, of each
bullet-eaten cave by the roadside—razed down to a crumpled papier-mâché.

my brother, ulcering out of my grip the way a blood-soaked font detaches
from the page of medical record as a pulsing illness, or a budding lump.

'tonight stinks like an open sore.' & in the wild gift of event, a scar
shapeshifts towards healing. violence scrawled in its wake.
& styling its way into turbulence—it thunders through a ribcage.

2.
there: the hurt, bruised to whitening. there: the chewed carnivorous
water—yawning a boneyard of flesh. the shore is language dead enough
to drown in, to squeeze to a thorough blot & punctuate with rumpled bodies
of my race. their negritude, whitewashed into effervescence.
our crude & grief-infested dialect like yellow bile, unsettling the tongue.

3.
post-war, a fragment of our surname drown in bulletproof soil. brother,
deboning the wild knit of concrete. he yanks off a body from its loamy
existence, & the air reeks of Ma. a boy ago, he grieved the dry season
of his infancy into a bonfire with no bones to hawk the flame.

amusement parks grew less amusing—slaughter driven by the urgency
for blood. carousel, racing same way into the tummy of an ambulance.

4.
the kill are smuggled in body bags on trolley, headed for nowhere.
grief grows surplus & doubles over with loss. a lad, foisted to a
stretcher—brandishes his dislodged wrist as a teenage gadget,
& grieved a purple sore boomeranging everywhere across town.

what bullet colors my accent? the impact, too sporadic to chew a whole
lineage. what language meets a bomb halfway between *beauty & boom?*

5:
lights-out: a soft shadow loiters the lone street, scavenging the bloodshot
yard for tampon. & in a sleight of hand, unshelves a pregnancy test-kit.
a sergeant pounds her from behind—as if I mean, without a gun.

[prenatal]: she binge slowly on the fat bile of loss. gloom, trellising her insteps.
[postnatal]: she craved fish stew on empty cartridge, bullet-shaped torso of
a lamb—marred in gunpowder. see how sorrow makes a carnivore of us.

beware of me. grief burdens my core. a fetus once there has gone missing
& not one blood to show for it.

6.
say: the ancestors has no hand in our woe. say: their spirit misjudges the bullet.
resurrect their ancient loin, for each fallen shape to plead in cold-blooded language.
say, I was the voice peeling the wind, there's the probability you'd find me un-alived
by a missile or near miss, or vowel explosion. my tongue: a dead language.
phoneme, plastered to my cheek. its cruel alphabet—liquifying my gum,
as sadness foams in maritime rage.
the saltless blessing, roaming in my mouth like rotten carcass.

7.
in the year of disaster, your ghost come home to roost on the eve of May:
an earthshattering sound—headed towards chaos. at the crack of dawn,
you're boar leaping toward light: a violence dead on arrival.
in a country that speaks fire, *'my joy is a dead language.'*
a dark accent, scrubbing grief on pink tongue.
the colonist's verb keep revamping more corners for us to die in.

I wear my mouth in reverse, & gun a pronoun down in one shot. cheers to
how we self-identify with hurt: a bullet for dodged bullet—in this ghastly language.

say, you find harm to outpace. thank the fitness of foot,
thank the femur & the calcium that fills it with tonight's horse race.

8.
there, my dead relatives unfurling like a peeled chorus.
their unrehearsed glow—putting light to guesswork.
dear brother, happiness is a far cry from here, & at the rough edge lies
a matchet moon—the way the sky slit supplication into sore throat.

you shape out, voiceless from the onslaught.
see, what troubles your larynx: medieval's wreckage.
a cannon ball, gunning for your lung.

CONTRIBUTORS

Nawaaz Ahmed is a transplant from Tamil Nadu, India. Before turning to writing, he was a computer scientist, researching search algorithms for Yahoo. He holds an MFA from University of Michigan, Ann Arbor, and is the recipient of residencies from Macdowell, VCCA, Yaddo, and Djerassi. His debut novel *Radiant Fugitives* (2021) was a finalist for the 2022 Pen/Faulkner Award and the Edmund White Award for Debut Fiction, was longlisted for The Center for Fiction First Novel Prize and the Aspen Literary Prize. He currently lives in Brooklyn.

Molly Anne Blumhoefer writes creative nonfiction, short fiction, poetry, and hybrid. Much of her work explores subcultures of urban life, military families, and religious trauma. She grew up in Minneapolis, Minnesota and currently lives with her partner in Albuquerque, New Mexico. Her work has been published in *Harpy Hybrid Review*, *Lind of Advance*, *Eclectica*, and more.

Jack Bordnick has been part of the creative art world for as long as he can remember, beginning as a product designer and establishing his own design business in New York, Santa Fe, and Europe. His sculptural images incorporate both surrealistic, mythological, and magical imagery, fabricated in textural metallic mixed-media assemblages.

Susan Calvillo is a Chinese/Mexican-American mother of 2020 twins and the author of *Excerpts From My Grocery List* (Beard of Bees). Her short works have appeared in *Zyzzyva*, *New American Writing*, *West Wind Review*, *Lumina*, *Cipactli*, and other charming magazines. Keep reading at susancalvillo.com, follow on TikTok @thatbeardlessbard, or simply watch her eat cake and plant cacti on Instagram @susan_calvillo.

K-Ming Chang is a Kundiman fellow, a Lambda Literary Award finalist, and a National Book Foundation 5 Under 35 honoree. She is the author of the *New York Times Book Review* Editors' Choice books *Bestiary* and *Gods of Want* (One World/Random House), and two forthcoming books, a novel titled *Organ Meats* (One World) and a novella titled *Cecilia* (Coffee House Press). She lives in California.

Mary Cisper is the author of *Dark Tussock Moth*, winner of the 2016 Trio Award and published by Trio House Press. Her poems and reviews have appeared in *Lana Turner*, *Denver Quarterly*, *Colorado Review*, *Interim*, *Newfound*, *Oversound*, *Terrain*, and elsewhere. A former analytical chemist, she lives in northern New Mexico.

Susan Michele Coronel lives in New York City. Her poems have appeared in publications including *Spillway 29*, *TAB Journal*, *The Inflectionist Review*, *Gyroscope Review*, *Prometheus Dreaming*, and *One Art*. In 2021, one of her poems was runner-up for the Beacon Street Poetry Prize, and another was a finalist in the Millennium Writing Awards. In the same year, she received a Pushcart nomination and was longlisted for the Sappho Prize. Her poetry manuscript was a finalist for Harbor Editions' Laureate Prize.

Rachel Deutsch's illustrations and writing have appeared in *The New Yorker* Daily Shouts, *McSweeney's*, *PRISM International*, *The Pinch*, and more. She lives in Montreal with her partner and two small kids.

Jose Hernandez Diaz is a 2017 NEA Poetry Fellow. He is the author of *The Fire Eater* (Texas Review Press, 2020). His work appears in *The American Poetry Review*, *Boulevard*, *Conduit*, *Crazyhorse*, *Georgia Review*, *Huizache*, *Iowa Review*, *The Journal*, *The Missouri Review*, *Poetry*, *Porter House Review*, *The Southern Review*, *Witness Magazine*, *The Yale Review*, and in *The Best American Nonrequired Reading Anthology 2011*. He teaches creative writing online and edits for *Frontier Poetry*.

Antony Fangary is a writer and visual artist living in San Francisco. He was awarded the 2023 National Endowment for the Arts Fellowship and is the author of *HARAM* (Etched Press, 2019). His poetry has recently appeared in *Gulf Coast*, *The Sycamore Review*, *West Branch*, and elsewhere. His work has received support from the San Francisco Arts Commission, Yerba Buena Center for the Arts, and the Center for Cultural Innovation.

Gloria Frimpong is a Ghanaian-American digital artist and creative writer.

She loves creating abstract art and writing stories and poetry, and is studying psychology to become a neuroscientist. She also creates short films in her free time, and is aspiring to become an independent filmmaker, specializing in psychological thrillers.

Lauren Brazeal Garza is a disabled writer, finishing her PhD in literature at the University of Texas at Dallas. Under the name Lauren Brazeal, her published poetry collections include *Gutter* (YesYes Books, 2018), which chronicles her homelessness as a teenager. She has also published two chapbooks. Her individual poems and essays have appeared or are forthcoming from *Poetry Northwest*, *Waxwing*, and *Verse Daily*, among many others.

A native of Ohio and a longtime resident of Alexandria, Egypt, **Jennifer Gauthier** was awarded a MacDowell fellowship in 2013. Her work has appeared in *South Dakota Review*.

John Kim wrote fanzines in the pre-Internet era and continued to do so well after. His writing can be found in *The Normal School*, *Juked*, and *The Southern Humanities Review*, among others. He has an MFA from UC Irvine and lives in Maryland with his family. His three most-listened-to punk records are "And Out Come the Wolves..." by Rancid, "Godammit" by Alkaline Trio, and "Reinventing Axl Rose" by Against Me!

Nicole Lachat was born in Edmonton, Canada to a Peruvian mother and Swiss father. She earned her MFA in creative writing from New York University. Her poetry appears in *Birdfeast Magazine*, *Palimpsest Magazine*, *Tinderbox Poetry Journal*, and *Ruminate Magazine*, among others. She was long-listed for the 2021 CBC Poetry Prize and currently lives in Lincoln, where she is pursuing her PhD in creative writing at the University of Nebraska.

Isaac George Lauritsen is a writer living in Chicago. His work can be found or is forthcoming in *Bennington Review*, *Denver Quarterly*, *DIAGRAM*, *Hobart Pulp*, *Inverted Syntax*, *Muzzle Magazine*, *Sidereal Review*, *TIMBER*, on a broadside from Octopus Books, and elsewhere. You can look at his photos and illustrations on Instagram: @ig_laurit.

Lauren Lavín's work appears in *Triangle House Review*, *Jarnal Vol. 1* (Mason Jar Press), *Sundog*, *The Hard Times: The First 40 Years* (Mariner Books), *Reductress*, and elsewhere. She was managing editor for the interactive fiction anthology *Los Suelos, CA* and is currently nonfiction editor for *Word West Revue*. She lives and collaborates with her husband in Seattle.

Claire Lawrence is a storyteller and mixed-media visual artist based in British Columbia. Her stories have appeared in numerous publications worldwide. In Canada, she has been published in *Geist*, *Pulp Literature*, and shortlisted for The Federation of BC Writers 2022 contest. She was nominated for the 2016 Pushcart Prize. Claire's art has been accepted by *Inverted Syntax*, *pulpMag*, *Black Lion Journal*, *Esthetic Apostle*, and *Sunspot*. She was a 2021 Best of the Net nominee for best artwork (cover). Her goal is to create and publish in all genres, and not inhale too many fumes.

Growing up in Southeast Louisiana, outside of New Orleans, **Shelbey Leco** was always inspired by nature. As a young adult, she studied at the University of New Orleans where she obtained her bachelor's degree in interdisciplinary studies in urban society with disciplines: education, English, and anthropology. She enjoys traveling, art, and exploring new places.

Writer and biologist **S.A. Leger**, originating from the Rocky Mountains of Colorado, lives with her wife and Dachshund in Newfoundland, Canada. She is an information designer by day and an ornithologist most other times. Her poems have most recently appeared in *The Dodge*, *Storm Cellar*, *Dunes Review*, *the tiny*, *Mantra Review*, and *Kestrel*, among others.

Bronte Lim is a writer and medical student based in Toronto, Ontario. She completed her bachelor's at Harvard University, where she studied English literature and chemistry. Her creative fiction has appeared in *The Harvard Advocate*, *Chicago Quarterly Review*, *Split Lip Magazine*, *The Iowa Review*, and is forthcoming in *Grist: A Journal of the Literary Arts*.

Luis Lopez-Maldonado is a Xicanx poeta, choreographer, and educator, born and raised in Southern California. He/They earned a bachelor of arts from the University of California at Riverside, in creative writing and dance. His/Their poetry has been seen in *The American Poetry Review*, *Foglifter*, *The Packinghouse Review*, *Public Pool*, and *Latina Outsiders: Remaking Latina Identity*, among many others. He/They also earned a master of arts in dance from Florida State University and a master of fine arts in creative writing from the University of Notre Dame, where he/they was/were poetry editorial assistant for *Notre Dame Review* and founder of the men's writing workshop in the St. Joseph County Juvenile Justice Center. Recipient of the Sparks Summer Fellowship 2016. He/They are currently adding his/their glitter to the Land of Enchantment, working for the public education system as a high school bilingual and special education teacher.

Richard Loranger is a multi-genre writer, performer, musician, visual artist, and all-around squeaky wheel currently residing in Oakland, CA. He is the founder of Poetea, a monthly literary conversation group. His upcoming collection of poetry and flash prose, *Mammal*, is due out from Roof Books in fall 2023. He's also the author of *Unit of Agency*, *Be A Bough Tit*, *Sudden Windows*, *Poems for Teeth*, *The Orange Book*, and ten chapbooks, and has work in over 100 magazines and journals. You can find more about his work and scandals at www.richardloranger.com.

Matthew Moniz is a PhD student of poetry at the University of Southern Mississippi. Originally from the DC area, he holds an MFA and MA from McNeese State University and a BA from Notre Dame. Among other national and international journals, Matt's work has appeared in *Crab Orchard Review*, *Meridian*, and *Tupelo Quarterly*. He has been awarded the SCMLA Poetry Prize and grown in workshops with Tin House and the Community of Writers.

Rémy Ngamije is a Rwandan-born Namibian writer and photographer. He is the founder, chairperson, and artministrator of Doek, an independent arts organization in Namibia supporting the literary arts. He is also the editor-in-chief of *Doek! Literary Magazine*, Namibia's first and only literary magazine, and the founder of the Bank Windhoek Doek Literary Awards and the Doek Literary Festival. His debut novel *The Eternal Audience Of One* was first published in South Africa by Blackbird Books and is available worldwide from Scout Press (S&S); it was honored with a Special Mention at the inaugural Grand Prix Panafricain De Litterature in 2022. He won the Africa Regional Prize of the 2021 Commonwealth Short Story Prize and was shortlisted for the AKO Caine Prize for African Writing in 2021 and 2020. He was longlisted and shortlisted for the 2020 and 2021 Afritondo Short Story Prizes, respectively. In 2019 he was shortlisted for Best Original Fiction by Stack Magazines. More of his work can be read at: remythequill.com

Timothy Nolan (he/him/his) is a writer and visual artist living in Palm Springs, California with his husband and their rescue dog, Scout. He has exhibited extensively for three decades and his work is in the collections of the DeYoung Museum of Art in San Francisco, and the Portland Art Museum in Oregon. He's been a fellow at Yaddo, Ucross, and Djerassi. Throughout the 1990s he wrote art reviews for *New Art Examiner* and *Artweek*, but turned to poetry, first as an artist-in-residence at Willapa Bay AiR in 2017, and then more seriously in this time of COVID. His work appears in *Rise Up Review*, and in *Flux*, an online anthology by Fifth Wheel Press.

Lauren Osborn is a writer, amateur entomologist, and PhD student in the English program at Oklahoma State University. Her writing has appeared, or is forthcoming, in *The Cincinnati Review* miCRo series, *DIAGRAM*, *The North American Review*, *Carve*, *Willow Springs*, and elsewhere. She lives and writes in Stillwater, Oklahoma with her family of tarantulas and other exotic pets. You can follow her on Twitter @Lauren_E_Osborn.

Robert Palmer graduated Summa Cum Laude from ASU with a degree in fine art (painting) in 2003. He has been shown in several shows throughout Utah and Arizona. In June 2022, Robert was featured at Tempe Gammage Auditorium. His recent subject matter revolves around landscape. Some works are inspired by places he visited, while others are inspired by places he imagined. Visit https://www.instagram.com/robert.palmer.7505/.

Hiram Perez teaches in the English Department at Vassar College. He is at work on a memoir that contemplates the relationships between racial embodiment, sexuality, and shame. His first book, *A Taste for Brown Bodies: Gay Modernity and Cosmopolitan Desire* (NYU Press), was awarded the Lambda Literary prize (or "Lammy") for LGBT Studies in 2016. He has published memoir in *Brevity*, *Tahoma Literary Review*, and *Burningword Literary Journal.*

Christopher Rodriguez is an undergraduate at CSU Stanislaus in Turlock, CA, earning a BFA in fine arts and a minor in gender studies. He is focused on exploring the duality of private spaces and the suburban façade, as well as sexuality, gender identity, and memory. A goal of his is to attend an MFA program with an emphasis in painting. He plans to use his learned skills to teach other artists painting and drawing.

Jewel Rodriguez is a painter residing in California's Central Valley. She is currently earning her BFA at California State University Stanislaus in Turlock, CA. Jewel uses her experiences from a tumultuous childhood as inspiration to create narrative scenes that discuss abuse, memory, and expectations of women in domestic environments.

Nnadi Samuel (he/him/his) holds a BA in English & literature from the University of Benin. He is the author of *Nature knows a little about Slave Trade* (Sundress Publications, 2023), winner of the Editor's Choice for publication, selected by Tate N. Oquendo. His work aims at amplifying marginalized voices. He won the 2021 International Human Rights Art Festival (IHRAF) award in New York, the 2022 River Heron Editor's Prize, and the 2022 bronze Creative Future Writers' Award in London, and is a three-time Best of the Net nominee and seven-time Pushcart Prize nominee. He tweets @Samuelsamba10.

Kurt Schweigman is Oglala/Sicangu Lakota, born and raised in South Dakota, and currently residing in Sonoma County, California. He is co-editor of *Red Indian Road West: Native American Poetry from California* (Scarlet Tanager, 2016). His new poetry book *Confluences of Solitude* (Mitote Press, 2023) is his first book in nearly a decade. Kurt's bilingual poetry book *Roots Define the Reach of My Branches* will be published by Gilgamesh Press (Mantua, Italy) in summer 2023. Currently, he is writing his first novel titled *Sitting Bull in Paris*, which is contemporary and historical fiction.

Dorsía Smith Silva is a four-time Pushcart Prize nominee, Best of the Net finalist, Best New Poets nominee, Cave Cavem Poetry Prize semifinalist, Obsidian Fellow, and full professor of English at the University of Puerto Rico, Río Piedras. Her poetry has been shortlisted for the Queen Mary Wasafiri New Writing Prize (2021) and has recently been published or is forthcoming in *Crazyhorse*, *Cream City Review*, *Poetry Northwest*, *The Minnesota Review*, *The Offing*, *Shenandoah*, and elsewhere. She is the author of *Good Girl* (micro-chapbook), editor of *Latina/Chicana Mothering*, and the co-editor of seven books. She has also attended the Bread Loaf Environmental Writers' Workshop, Bread Loaf Writers' Workshop, Tin House Workshop, and the Kenyon Review Writers' Workshop. Lastly, she has a PhD in Caribbean Literature and posts on Twitter as @DSmithSilva.

Ronita Sinha resides in Toronto, Canada. She is a traveler, recipe experimenter, and gardener, tilling her soul for words and images, and when she cannot help it, she writes. She holds an MPhil degree in English literature from Calcutta, India. She has been shortlisted by *Sixfold Literary Magazine* in their annual fiction contests in 2021 and 2022 and published in print and online as one of the top fifteen. She was a finalist for Globe Soup's annual short story contest in July 2021. Her work has appeared in *East of the Web*, *The Academy of the Heart and Mind*, *The Other Side of Hope*, and *The Literary Yard*. In August 2020, she was awarded "Storyteller of the Month" by The Magic Diary. Ronita is a fiction reader for *Atticus Review*.

Krystle May Statler (she/her) is a Black multiracial artist living in Portland, OR. Her artwork is featured in the *Black Women for Wellness* and *New Black City: A World Without Police* exhibits. Her poems and essays are featured in *1455's Movable Type*, *The Santa Fe Writers Project Quarterly*, *Cultural Weekly*, or are forthcoming. Krystle's debut poetic-visual hybrid, *Losing Blood*, was a finalist for the 2021 CAAPP Book Prize. Visit www.krystlemaystatler.com.

A.P. Thayer is a queer, Mexican-American author based out of Los Angeles who writes nightmarism and cross-genre speculative fiction. His work has been published in places like *Dark Matter Magazine*, *Space Fantasy Magazine*, and *Uncharted Magazine*, as well as in several anthologies. He is also a member of SFWA and HWA. Find his published work, social media information, and blog at www.apthayer.com/links.

Hailing from Los Angeles and currently living in South Korea, **Nathan Truong** is an interdisciplinary writer working at the intersections of travel and culture. He is inspired by memory and social formations of social unease. His practice explores avenues for forging more-than-human relations for mutual flourishing. He can be contacted at www.natktruong.info.

Angelica Whitehorne has published work in *Westwind Poetry*, *Mantis*, *Air/Light Magazine* and *The Laurel Review*, among others. She is the author of the chapbook *The World Is Ending, Say Something That Will Last* (Bottle Cap Press, 2022). Besides being a devastated poet, she is a marketing content writer for a green energy loan company, and a volunteer reader for Autumn House Press.

Don Zancanella is the recipient of the Iowa Short Fiction Award and an O. Henry Prize. One of his stories was cited as a distinguished story of the year in *Best American Short Stories 2019*, and he has been published widely in literary magazines. His books include a collection of stories, *Western Electric* (Univ. of Iowa Press), and three novels, *Concord* (Serving House Books), *A Storm in the Stars* (Delphinium), and *Animals of the Alpine Front* (coming from Delphinium in 2024).

Lena Zycinsky is an artist and poet. Her work can be found online at www.lenazycinsky.com.

The Editors would like to thank the following Bay Area retailers for carrying *Fourteen Hills*:

BERKELEY
Pegasus Books

OAKLAND
East Bay Booksellers
Walden Pond Books

SAN FRANCISCO
Dog Eared Books
Green Apple Books
Medicine for Nightmares
Needles & Pens
West Portal Bookshop

SAN JOSE
Recycle Bookstore

SAUSALITO
Sausalito Books by the Bay

SEBASTOPOL
Copperfield's Books

think *yours* is good?
submit!

February 15th – June 15th
https://fourteenhills.submittable.com*

visual art • experimental •
fiction • poetry • creative nonfiction

more info., guidelines, interviews, essays:
www.14hills.net

for issues & purchases, please visit:
www.spdbooks.org

*For those without computer access, please mail your completed, neatly-printed manuscript with your name and contact information *year-round* to:

Fourteen Hills Press
SFSU Creative Writing Dept.
1600 Holloway Ave
San Francisco CA 94132

"Beautifully designed, impeccably edited, *Fourteen Hills* is one of those handful of literary journals doing the important work of keeping American writing alive and new."
—**George Saunders**

"*Fourteen Hills* might just as aptly be titled 'Fourteen Styles,' such a broad spectrum of approaches to narrative and poetics does it present."
—**Mark Cunningham, NewPages.com**

"That *Fourteen Hills* is able to consistently put together books full of quality and grace always astonishes me."
—**Stephen Elliott**